Lemon Filled Disaster

D0873223

LEMON FILLED DISASTER

Tyora Moody

Tymm Publishing LLC
Columbia, SC

Lemon Filled Disaster
A Eugeena Patterson Mystery, Book 3

Copyright © 2018 by Tyora Moody

All rights reserved. No part of this book may be reproduced or transmitted in any form or by any means without written permission of the author.

Lemon Filled Disaster is a work of fiction. Names, characters, places and incidents either are products of the author's imagination or are used fictitiously. Any resemblance to actual persons, living or dead, events, or locales is entirely coincidental.

Paperback ISBN-13: 978-0-9984569-6-6
ePub ISBN-13: 978-0-9984569-7-3

Published by Tymm Publishing LLC
701 Gervais Street, Suite 150-185
Columbia, SC 29201
www.tymmpublishing.com

Cover Design: TywebbinCreations.com
Cover Illustration: lifestealer, fiverr.com
Copy Editing/Proofreading: Felicia Murrell

Chapter 1

The moist lemon flavored cake captivated my taste buds. The sweetness was satisfying but not overpowering. I plunged the plastic white fork into the cake to savor yet another bite of goodness. I felt a smile tug at my cheeks, which meant I was really grinning up something awful.

In the past five years, I'd become a widow, an empty nester, retired after thirty years of teaching middle school and struggled daily with my greatest comfort — food. My sweet tooth and desire for carbs had slowly become my enemy, leaving me with this battle to monitor my blood sugar every day. I'd lost over fifty pounds in the past two years, but still craved all the food I'd lost on the journey. As a recently acquired wedding planner, I was happy this errand turned out to be a great start for a Tuesday. But there was so much left to do, even for my retiree schedule.

I looked down at the table where two other plates sat in front of me. I'd almost forgot to try the other wedding cake samples. I stuck my fork into the other two prepared slices. One plate held a yellow cake with fluffy buttercream icing. It tasted like any other cake I had in my lifetime. Nothing extraordinary, but definitely too sweet. On the other plate was a two-layer white angel food cake with a thin layer of strawberries in between the layers. Neither could top the first sample. The light lemon cake was a masterpiece.

I looked over at my future daughter-in-law, Dr. Carmen Alpine. "Carmen, this one tastes so good. Are you sure this is okay for me to be eating?"

Carmen's eyes looked glazed over as if her mind had been transported away from Sweet Dreams Bakery. The independent boutique bakery took on a limited number of clients, and we were lucky to be squeezed in today. I peered down at the plates in front of Carmen and noticed she hadn't tasted any of the cake selections. I nudged her. "Carmen, are you okay? We have to make this decision today in order to have the cake ready for October twenty-second."

She blinked, as if I'd awaken her. "Yes, you're right." She grabbed a fork and scooped up the lemon cake from the plate in front of her.

I watched as she quietly tasted each cake slice almost like a robot. I knew Carmen had worked a long shift at the hospital yesterday. I wasn't sure if she was tired or if something else was on her mind. Last year, Carmen had completed her residency where she'd met my son, Dr. Cedric Patterson. Both of them were obstetricians. Cedric had officially brought Carmen into his thriving private practice and his heart. Almost forty, my bachelor son had finally found a business partner as well as the love of his life. This woman who I'd grown to accept as a member of the family was a decade younger than my son and just as tall as him too. Carmen reminded me of the singer Beyoncé except she wore her honey blonde tresses in a natural do. Today, her hair was pulled high on her head in a curly puff.

Neither Carmen or Cedric had time to do wedding planning. Both were quite alright with going to the justice of peace in their scrubs and calling it a day, but Carmen's parents and I objected, insisting on a wedding ceremony. I'd waited so long to see Cedric find someone. Unlike his older brother, Junior, who married his college sweetheart, I was starting to think Cedric despised the institution of marriage. I mailed a batch of invitations for the busy couple yesterday. We might just make it through these wedding plans without any trouble, even though we were way behind on the checklist.

Carmen swallowed the last piece of cake and turned towards me. "I asked the chef to create something that tasted good but wouldn't send people's blood sugar sky high. She mentioned something about using Stevia and applesauce to substitute for the sugar."

I grinned again. "Well, she did a good job. I need to remember that combination the next time I bake. Now will she do this as a two tier or three tier cake?"

Though her body was still sitting next to me in the bakery, Carmen seemed to wander off again.

Okay, I was becoming concerned. There was something about Carmen's slumped posture that didn't denote an excited bride.

"Are you upset because Cedric couldn't make it to the cake testing? You of all people should know babies don't wait to be delivered."

Carmen's flushed face appeared as if she was going to burst into tears. I watched as she shut her eyes and then opened them. The smooth, caramel complexion of her face seemed composed, but her large brown eyes remained tormented. "No, one of us had to be at the practice today. Cedric does have a patient who can deliver any time now. I'm happy to have you along, Ms. Eugeena. You've been really great with all this wedding planning."

When I first met Carmen, I wasn't so sure about this relationship between a doctor and his resident. But over time, since she became the only woman in a long line of prospects my son solidly committed to, Carmen had won me over.

Now I just needed to work on my youngest and only daughter, Leesa, a mother of two who had yet to marry. I continued to pray for the right man to come along. Leesa had jumped wholeheartedly into planning the reception for her brother and future sister-in-law, and it did my heart good to see her embrace her favorite brother's wedding.

I blew out a breath and started to ask Carmen again about the cake, but Chef Ruth Cordell came around the corner with her hands clasped. "So how was it?" The chef looked at the samples in front of Carmen. "Which one did you like?"

Carmen glanced up at the chef. She reached down and grabbed a fork and stuck it into the plate with the lemon cake. As Carmen chewed thoughtfully, a slight smile appeared on her face. "This is it? Don't you think, Eugeena?"

I nodded, happy to see Carmen had snapped out of whatever had been bothering her.

She nodded, "I'd like to have a two-tiered cake for the cake on display, as well as a sheet cake for backup."

The chef jotted notes on her pad. "Got it. We'll add your cake to our calendar. The big day is October twenty-second, correct?"

"Yes," Carmen responded, her voice low.

The pastry chef glanced at me, and I smiled.

After Chef Cordell walked back towards the kitchen, I raised my eyebrow at Carmen's soft-spoken response. There was something else going on with Carmen that had nothing to do with being tired after a long shift. I prodded. "Is everything okay with you and Cedric?"

She looked at me, her eyes appeared sad. "Yes, we're fine."

"How come you don't sound like you're fine? If I didn't know better, I would think you're just going through the motions. I know this can all be overwhelming. Are you having second thoughts?"

She shook her head. "No. I just have something on my mind. Something came up unexpectedly, and I'm still trying to wrap my head around it. I'll be fine. I appreciate you and Leesa helping me with the wedding. I don't know what I would do without you both."

"Well, let's get some lunch. I'm feeling a bit low and a meal may do us both some good." I rose from the chair to stretch my legs. During the hot, summer months, I'd not been diligent to keep up with my walking. I could feel extra pounds on me that I didn't need. September still had some muggy days, but at least I was attempting to rise a bit early to get in a walk around the neighborhood. Thankfully, I'd walked this morning. Getting old came with an annoying stiffness that walking helped relieve.

When the chef came out to consult with Carmen about the cake invoice, I headed towards the front of the bakery. Sweet aromas had assaulted my nose from the time we entered, and I figured taking a peek at the offerings didn't hurt. My eyes zoned on a large cheese danish with tiny pecans embedded in the icing. Cheese danish had been my vice for years. I would have one almost every morning with black coffee before starting my day teaching South Carolina history to eighth graders.

I caught sight of Carmen coming from the back room, thankfully saving me from the tortuous temptations. I turned to ask her if she was ready to go when I noticed her face. She was staring out the window at something or someone.

The door to the bakery opened with the jingle of a bell.

I rotated my body to see a man walk through the doors. His eyes were focused on Carmen. The man was tall, probably over six feet. His skin was a deep dark brown and his eyes were almond shaped. He had the kind of lashes many women strived to achieve with mascara. He spoke, his voice hoarse as if he hadn't used his vocal chords in a long time or was a possible smoker. "Carmen, it's good to see you again."

Again? Who was this man and how did he know Carmen?

Carmen brushed past me towards the door. "Ms. Eugeena, we need to go."

"Okay." I glanced at the man whose face looked as though Carmen had punched him. I hurried behind Carmen. Her long legs seemed to have forgotten the old woman behind her.

I called out. "Carmen, slow down. What's your hurry?"

I found myself sprinting as Carmen reached her silver Nissan Murano. Before I arrived, she'd already unlocked the doors with her key fob and climbed into the driver's seat.

Was she going to leave me?

I rushed around the car and snatched open the passenger door just as Carmen cranked the engine. Out of breath, I hefted my body inside the car. It took what felt like several minutes to catch my breath. I looked at her.

"Thank you for the impromptu exercise. Would you mind telling me what's going on with you today?"

I turned around to look through the back window. The man who Carmen seemed to be running from was standing outside the bakery staring at us. "Carmen, who is that man? Why is he looking at us?"

Carmen glanced at her rear-view mirror. "We need to get out of here now."

I reached for the seat belt and fastened it as Carmen lurched the car into reverse. She tore out of the parking lot, burning rubber. I tightened my seatbelt and clung to the door rest. "Carmen," I shrieked, "Are you trying to give me a heart attack?"

Carmen's shoulders dropped. "I'm sorry, Ms. Eugeena. I'm so sorry."

I loosened my grip on the car door and tried to calm myself. "How about we get some real food to eat? I think you owe me an explanation, young lady."

Carmen nodded her head and drove quietly. She gripped the steering wheel so hard I thought she would break it.

Ten minutes later, she turned the car into Charleston Good Eats, a new family-owned restaurant. It was a popular eatery, especially during the lunch hour, and after much circling, Carmen found a parking space near the back. Looking like a little girl who'd lost her favorite toy, she didn't immediately cut the engine. I could see she was visibly shaking.

"Do you want to tell me what's going on?"

"I don't know if I can. I don't know if I deserve you caring so much or even Cedric's love at this point."

I frowned. I expected tears and drama from my

daughter. Watching the usual stoic Carmen break down concerned me. "Carmen, tell me what's going on."

She wiped the tears streaming down her face with her sleeve.

I reached over and rubbed her arm. "What's got you so upset? You know you can talk to me. Who was the man back there at the bakery?"

Carmen lifted her eyes to the top of the car roof as though she sought God for support. "Ms. Eugeena, I haven't been truthful. I've been trying to keep my past behind me, but it's managed to catch up with me. That...that...that man...was...my ex-husband."

I clutched my chest. I was trying not to make a Fred Sanford move because that would be overly dramatic on my part, but my heart jolted with fear.

Was this young woman whom I accepted about to break my son's heart?

Chapter 2

It took me a minute to remember to breathe. Good thing Carmen had left the air condition running. I reached for the air vent to make sure it was blowing full blast on my burning hot face. It was early September, but Charleston, South Carolina, didn't know anything about cooling down. Fall and spring always went through the South like a blur, barely noticeable. Summertime humidity seemed to stick around until it lost the battle with winter. Even then, winter barely took a bite of the South.

I looked over at Carmen and asked, "Does Cedric know you were married before?"

She shook her head. "No. I've been meaning to tell him, but the words never come. Now Darius is here in town. I'm still in shock after not seeing him for so many years."

I frowned. Carmen was only twenty-eight. She must have married this man pretty young.

"So your ex-husband just shows up in town all of a sudden?"

"He found me. Darius Randall found me." Her voice lowered but was still intense. "He called me this morning.

I don't even know how he got my number." She seemed to be gulping for air. "But he's been in Charleston since last week. I saw him last Thursday at the hospital. It was like seeing a ghost. He just appeared casually in front of me, smiling as if he'd been a part of my life all this time." Carmen's voice cracked.

"Just breathe, honey. It's going to be okay." I prayed Carmen wouldn't hyperventilate on me. I'd never seen her like this before.

"It was a mistake to marry him," she practically whispered.

"Well, I suppose you were in love with him at one time. Love has been known to fool a person. You had to be pretty young, right?"

She nodded. "I was seventeen when I met him. He seemed so grown-up, more mature than the boys my age. After a few months of being with him, I found myself pregnant. I had just turned eighteen."

A child? "Oh." *What else was she going to spring on me?* "You have a child too?"

"I lost the baby." Carmen closed her eyes. "Darius pushed me, and I fell down a flight of stairs. He made me lose the baby."

I flinched from the anguish in Carmen's voice. I knew about marrying young. Ralph Patterson and I married shotgun style when my family found out I was pregnant with Junior. For many years, I resented my marriage. Thankfully, God moved Ralph and I to reconcile a few years before his passing, but I couldn't imagine a man placing his hands on me and causing such devastating harm.

"It sounds like you needed to get away from Darius." I tried to remember the man's face I'd just seen moments ago before we rushed away. "He doesn't sound like a nice man."

Carmen sniffed. "I stayed with him a few months after the baby died. I should've left sooner. He blamed me for losing the baby when he was the one who pushed me." She scoffed, "He claimed I was standing too close to the edge. The man placed both hands squarely on my back and shoved me. It took me a few months, but my parents helped me get a divorce lawyer."

She let out a breath as if pushing the memories away. "My parents felt like I was too young and influenced by an older man. The divorce was almost painless. Darius didn't put up a huge fuss. He wanted to be rid of me. I went off to college like I was supposed to, graduated, completed medical school, entered residency. Then I met Cedric."

Carmen looked at me. "Ms. Eugeena, I put Darius behind me. I didn't mean to keep this from Cedric. I just pushed that whole part of my life out of my mind."

I rubbed her arm. "I understand. If I were your parents, I would have done the same thing to get you out of that awful marriage. You know you need to tell Cedric. He's thinking you both are getting married for the first time. He needs to know."

"I know, but I'm afraid Cedric will not accept this with an open heart."

"Cedric loves you. Believe me, I know my son. You tell him what you told me. He'll understand. Now can we get some food? I think I'm going to pass out." I wasn't being overly dramatic either. My face was feeling sweaty despite the air conditioning.

"Oh, yes, I'm sorry. We need to take care of you."

Carmen and I was seated for our meal, and I checked my glucose which was definitely low. I swallowed a glucose tablet and drank the water Carmen had requested from the waiter.

After we received our orders, we both seemed to get back to normal. That was as normal as one can be after learning about Carmen's past. I polished off my grilled chicken salad and realized telling Carmen my son would understand could be wishful thinking. I knew my middle child very well. Cedric's sensitivity could make him react in a way that was not good. One of the reasons why Cedric had remained a bachelor so long was his determination to not be hurt by a woman. He played the field and pretended to enjoy his life, but when I saw Cedric with his nephews and niece, I saw the family man he longed to become one day.

One could only hope and pray.

Carmen took care of the bill. As we headed back to the car, something caught my attention from the side.

Was that Darius Randall looking at us from across the parking lot?

I looked over at Carmen who seemed to be in better spirits. She hadn't noticed what I saw. We climbed back into the car. I looked in the passenger side mirror, and then pulled down the visor to peer through the mirror. Mr. Randall wasn't in sight, but I was thoroughly creeped out. It's possible I was seeing things, but my age hadn't stopped my ability to pick up details.

Darius Randall appeared to be following us. Carmen not only needed to tell Cedric, she may need to report this man to the police. This man came to Charleston for a reason and seemed determined to talk to Carmen.

Chapter 3

My nerves were fraught when I woke up the next morning. I dreamed Cedric called off the wedding and didn't sleep as peacefully as I hoped. I threw off the covers and lifted my body to a sitting position. The sunlight was peeking strongly through the blind. On the other side of my bedroom, my roommate, a very round Corgi, raised his eyes to look at me but didn't move from his doggy bed. Porgy knew once my feet hit the floor it was time to get some nibbles.

Ralph had never let the children own a pet. Two years ago, after the untimely death of an old friend and neighbor, Mary Fleming, I inherited Porgy. Or rather, he chose me as his new owner. I was still saddened by Mary's death, especially since I was the one who found her. I also happened to be the one to discover her killer too. Retirement had been quite an adventure for me, but lately it had become quiet. The hair on my arm prickled as though something was telling me the quietness would soon change.

Today was Wednesday, my day to work the afterschool

program at Missionary Baptist Church. I still had plenty of time to myself before heading out to open the church in the afternoon. I was tempted to call Cedric's house where he and Carmen shared a home. Shacking as they would say in my day. I have to admit I was happy about the engagement making their sharing a home more official.

It was probably best to wait and let the couple work it out. I thought of two people I could talk to about what was ailing me. My aunt Cora, who was more like a sister since we were only two years apart. She was the last child birthed by my grandparents right around the time my dad had me. Lately, she was caught up taking care of her oldest sister, Aunt Esther. How the oldest and the youngest child were still left out of eight children was amazing since the two women were quite alike in many ways. I knew this early in the morning wouldn't be a good time to call.

The next person on my list was my next-door neighbor. He probably was the better choice, mainly because I rather liked his company. Amos Jones and I have solved other mysteries together, and I was starting to think this man from Carmen's past was indeed a mysterious one.

Why did he show up out of the blue, now? Carmen mentioned she saw him last week at the hospital. I wondered if it had anything to do with Carmen's upcoming wedding. The past had a way of rearing its head when a person was trying to move towards the future.

I grabbed the phone and asked Amos if he would join me for breakfast. He never declined any of my meal invitations, and this morning was no different. I must say I never expected I would prepare meals for another man after losing Ralph almost five years ago. But over the years, Amos and I had become friends. Some folks like Carmen, Leesa and Cora claimed he may as well be my boyfriend.

I was far too old for that nonsense, plus I liked the word *companion* better.

Amos was a retired detective and also a widow. His wife succumbed to breast cancer not too long after Ralph's heart attack carried him away. Unlike me, where my children all still lived in South Carolina, Amos's children lived around the country and rarely kept in touch with him. It was a conversation I tried to approach with him, but I often hit a wall. I knew he was hurt by the distance between his daughters and grandchildren. My family had accepted him, and he seemed to enjoy hanging around us.

By the time Amos arrived, I had taken a quick shower, dressed in a short sleeve blue maxi dress and placed turkey bacon in the oven. I wore an apron over my dress to keep it clean since it would serve me all day. I wouldn't have tried this style of dress if not for my daughter, Leesa. She turned me onto it. The dress reached my ankles but didn't feel like I was wearing a sheet. It moved with me as I walked keeping me comfortable and cool for yet another muggy September day in the South.

Amos grinned as I opened the door, probably excited from the smells wafting from the kitchen. Of course, I'd also noticed how his eyes swept over me and the way his brown eyes, gazed back at me like I was the most important person in the world. Once he stepped inside, he must have sensed my nervous mood because he raised an eyebrow. "Uh oh, let me guess, there's trouble brewing in your brain."

I swatted at him. "Not anything bad that would require police intervention." I had stumbled into two crime scenes in the past two years. I was a retired social studies teacher, but somehow, I'd found myself solving murders. That wasn't what I had in mind all those years ago when I thought about what I would do after I retired from the classroom.

As Amos followed me towards the kitchen, something about yesterday flashed into my mind. *Darius was following us yesterday. Was he a danger to Carmen?* Before Amos could sit at the table, I gasped and grabbed his arm. "I may have spoken too soon about police intervention."

Amos shook his head. "Let me sit down for this. A sixth sense warned me that you didn't just call me over for breakfast for no reason."

I shrunk back. "I have fixed meals for you plenty of times."

"Not since you started this wedding planning business with Carmen."

I turned my eyes towards the ceiling, thinking that couldn't be true. I went over to the stove to stir the grits. "Well, I'm not trying to avoid you. Cedric and Carmen sprang this October twenty-second date on us during the fourth of July picnic. End of August, when I asked them how the wedding planning was going, both said neither of them could find the time outside of their patients. Women have babies all the time and they need their doctors. When I heard they were considering going to the justice of the peace, I just couldn't handle that."

I huffed. "Do you know how long I've been waiting on another wedding in this family? Junior has been married twelve years now. My two youngest children don't seem to care about marriage. I was starting to think maybe Ralph and I had been a bad influence."

Amos frowned. "People spend an enormous amount of money on weddings and seem to forget the importance of the marriage part. I should know. I spent $10,000 on my oldest daughter's wedding. Then she and the guy divorced barely three years later. It's good that young people take their time."

I raised my eyebrow. Amos rarely shared information about his daughters. Seemed like they would have been more grateful to him. Growing up with a dad who was often missing and tied up in police cases, Amos felt the girls just didn't know him.

It was a shame. Sometimes people didn't know how to let go of grudges.

I grabbed four eggs out of the refrigerator and proceeded to crack them in a bowl. I added a little bit of ground pepper and then whisked the eggs. The entire time I scrambled the eggs in my favorite cast iron skillet, my mind kept going back to yesterday. "Amos, what can the police do about a stalker?"

Amos raised his bushy eyebrow at me. "You have one?"

"No, not me!" I sighed. "I guess I better start from the beginning. Yesterday, this guy shows up at the bakery where Carmen and I were taste-testing wedding cake. Oh, the cake is going to be so good, by the way. Anyway, Carmen was acting awfully funny the whole time, then this guy shows up. Carmen took one look at him, and the next thing I knew we were practically running for the car like our lives were in danger."

I stopped my tirade long enough to turn the top and bottom stove off. I wasn't about to burn the food while telling Amos what happened.

I turned around to face him. "Come to find out, *that man* was her ex-husband. Anyway, from the way Carmen told it, he was not a good guy at all. He sounded abusive. Thankfully, I calmed her down and we had lunch. But here's the thing, that gave me the creeps. I could've sworn when we left the restaurant that I saw the man again. He had to be following us!"

Amos's eyes were wide. "First of all, you kind of confused me with Carmen's ex-husband, the abuse, etc. Did you know she was married before?"

I thought it best to save the food and placed on my oven mitts, pulling the pan of bacon out of the oven before my storytelling skills kicked in again. I slowly removed the mitts and turned to face Amos. "No. I had no idea. She hadn't told Cedric either, and that has me worried. I don't know how my son is going to react, and I haven't heard anything yet. I hope he sees that she got mixed up with a man when she was way too young."

I was in overdrive. My thoughts and mouth were moving, but that wasn't stopping me from getting breakfast ready. All of this worrying had me hungry.

I took down some plates and placed the hot food on the table. "This man, Darius something. No wait, I think Carmen said Darius Randall. I don't understand why he showed up now." I sat and threw up my hands. "I don't know whether I should be more worried about this guy sneaking around or whether there is going to be a wedding at all?"

I looked at the table. "Oh, I didn't get us any utensils to eat with. Do you want some coffee?"

Amos held up his hands. "Let me get it, Eugeena. I think you need to calm your nerves."

I watched as Amos walked right over to the kitchen drawer that held the forks and then to the top kitchen cabinet. He took down two large white mugs. It occurred to me that Amos knew his way around my kitchen quite well. I can't say it bothered me, it was actually a bit of a comfort.

Ralph would have never offered.

Amos brought two steaming cups of coffee back to the table. We served ourselves and then ate in peace. At least until my cell phone rang.

My heart started beating fast. I looked over at Amos who stared at me as though to ask, *Are you going to answer that?*

I looked at the phone and saw Carmen's pretty face smiling back at me. I really liked the iPhone and other tech toys my children pitched in to give me, but sometimes it felt like I was in a twilight zone to see how these toys worked. I picked up on the second ring. "Hello. Carmen?"

"Eugeena, I can't get Cedric on the phone."

I frowned. "What do you mean? Did you talk to him last night?"

"I did. He was really upset. I don't know what to think. He left the house and didn't come back this morning. I need your help."

"Have you checked the hospital?"

Carmen wailed. "I've called everywhere. I'm so sorry to call you, but... I don't know what to do. I need to know where he is."

My mind tried to understand Carmen's anguish. It occurred to me there was something more going on than trying to find Cedric. "Carmen, where are you?"

I could hardly hear her breathing on the other end.

"Carmen, are you there? Please tell me where you are. I'll do my best to find Cedric."

"Ms. Eugeena, the cops are here now. Please, find Cedric for me."

I shot up from my chair, practically knocking it to the floor. "What? Wait a minute! What do you mean the cops are there now? Where are you? Carmen, talk to me."

"He's dead. Darius is dead. At least he can't bother me anymore."

The line went dead, and my mouth fell open. Amos stood from his chair, staring at me. "Eugeena? What did Carmen say?"

"Oh my gosh, I don't know what to think. That guy is dead. Carmen said the cops just showed up. We've got to find Cedric. Right now!"

But where was Carmen?

Chapter 4

Thank goodness Amos drove. I pressed Cedric's phone number over and over again, but all I kept getting was his voicemail. Cedric often stayed on call at the hospital since he was always delivering babies. No matter how upset he was at Carmen, he would be available for his patients. If I called him and he couldn't get to the phone, I always left a message for him. Cedric was good about calling back or better yet, showing up at my house.

"What should we do? I don't know whether to find Cedric or check on Carmen." A thought had occurred to me as soon as Carmen said Darius was dead, but I couldn't bring myself to focus on the thought.

"If Carmen was worried about Cedric, maybe we should find him." As though he could read my mind, Amos asked the unthinkable. "Do you think Cedric would have gotten angry enough to go after that man?"

"No! Cedric didn't even know the man. That's not Cedric. He would go off in a corner somewhere to think, but he wouldn't do anything impulsive."

Amos nodded as though to reassure me. "The police are

going to want to know both Carmen and Cedric's alibis. I will find out what I can from the police department. I still have some buddies over there."

"I do know Cedric spends the night at the hospital if he has a patient in labor. Maybe if we swing by there, we can find him."

"Sounds like a plan." Amos merged into I-526 traffic to head out towards Bon Secours St. Francis Hospital. He found a parking space at the hospital and turned to me. "I'll make some calls out here. You go find your son."

He didn't have to tell me twice. I was sprinting towards the hospital door as though I was in medical trouble, but my emergency was a little different. I headed straight to the elevators. There were a few others waiting for the elevator to go up. I tried to remain calm, but my breakfast was turning cartwheels in my stomach.

Seniority was in my favor when the elevator arrived because the others waited for me to step on first. Going on what I knew about my son, I pressed the number for the maternity floor. Cedric was a sensitive soul who didn't get along with his father at all. It was ironic that he was the one to follow in Ralph Patterson's footsteps. My eldest son, Ralph Patterson, Jr., better known as Junior to everyone, followed his own path and became a lawyer.

Ralph had been an obstetrician at the old Charleston Memorial Hospital for thirty years and created quite a legacy before he passed. Though Cedric had stepped into his father's role, he made his own mark. Like father, like son. They were trusted doctors delivering thousands of babies.

As soon as the doors opened, I walked purposefully towards the nurse's station. I had known many nurses in my time. They were a sharp crew who could tell you anything you needed to know. It was their duty to look after their patients which also meant keeping up with the doctor as well.

Head Nurse Maddy O'Donnell was barking out orders to three nurses at the station. I walked directly towards her. If anyone knew where Cedric was, it would be Nurse Maddy. She'd been at the hospital when Ralph was still alive.

She looked up as I approached, a smile stretching across her stern face. "Mrs. Patterson, it's been awhile since I've seen you. Don't you look good? Retirement is certainly agreeing with you."

"It's the best thing ever to finally have time for oneself." I tried to smile back, pretending like I wasn't going out of mind. "Would you happen to know where my son is? My future daughter-in-law and I are trying to track him down."

"Oh yes, we're all so excited about the upcoming wedding. Who knew someone would finally snatch the bachelor?"

"Yes, I know. Do you know where he is?"

"He was sleeping in the resident's room. Looked like he'd been there all night. He has Mrs. Hanson on his list today, but she's only dilated two inches so far. Looks like a long labor for that woman."

"Sounds like it. Can you point me in the right direction?"

"I'll walk you back there."

"Bless you, Maddy. I appreciate this so much, thanks."

I followed Maddy towards the back, hoping not to walk all over her feet in my hurry to get to Cedric. *If he'd been sleeping all this time, did he know what poor Carmen was going through right now?* I also hoped more nurses than Maddy noticed Cedric was here at the hospital. Before I arrived at the door, I asked, "Maddy, did Carmen call here?"

Maddy arched her eyebrow with questions in her eyes. "She may have left a message at the nurse's station. Is everything alright?"

"Yes." I forced a smile that was not matching with my twisting insides.

Maddy knocked on the door and then pushed it open. The room was dark except for a lamp in the corner of the room. Cedric sat upright on the edge of one of the beds in the room. He looked up, his eyes looking worn out as though he hadn't slept. "Mom, what are you doing here?"

"Looking for you." I shot a glance over at Maddy who seemed very interested in our conversation. The last thing we needed was for the nurses to be spreading gossip. "Thank you, Maddy, for helping me find him."

Maddy grinned. "Certainly. Dr. Patterson, I will keep you updated on Mrs. Hanson's progress. Right now, she's slowly dilating."

Cedric stood and stretched. "Thanks, Maddy."

Maddy closed the door as she left the room, and I turned to examine my son. He was usually meticulous about shaving, so this was the first time I noticed the gray in his beard which was moving past the five o'clock shadow phase. He wore scrubs and his white coat was thrown across the chair.

"Have you spoken to Carmen?"

He shook his head. "Not since last night. I needed to ... take a breather."

"So she told you about her ex-husband?"

Cedric frowned. "How did you know about that?"

"I met him yesterday. He's a creepy man. I think he may have been following us or something. Maybe I should have told Carmen to go to the police yesterday. She was really terrified of him."

Cedric's face looked conflicted. "She told me what he did to her. I just wished she'd said something earlier. Two years of being together and not once did she mention him. What do you mean he was following you?"

I shook my head, "That part isn't important at the moment. Carmen really needs you. I think she's frantic to make sure you didn't do anything rash. You did come straight to the hospital after you left home last night, right?"

"No, I drove around for a while. I just thought it would be good to be near my patients. I checked on two patients, looked in the nursery and then I came in here and tried to sleep. I guess I got some sleep. Not much." Cedric threw up his hands. "Mom, what's going on?"

"Then you don't know?"

He eyed me. "Know what, Mom?"

"Darius Randall is dead, and Cedric, you need to come up with a better timeline than that."

He jumped up. "What? How did he die?"

"I have no idea. We need to get to Carmen. When she called, she said the police had shown up. But she didn't tell me where she was."

Cedric frowned. "How did she know he was dead? Did she go see him?"

I shrugged. "I don't know. Why don't you call her and find out?"

Cedric looked around on the bed and grabbed his phone. "My phone is dead." He slapped the bed. "Can you call her?"

I'd already reached into my purse for my phone and

started the call. My son may have been an outstanding doctor, but sometimes I wondered about him.

I was also pondering if the one we should be more worried about was Carmen. She was a tall, athletic-looking woman, and I didn't doubt for a minute that if she needed to, she could handle herself. When I first met her, she struck me as a woman with a tough attitude. But I saw another side of Carmen yesterday that I had only seen a few other times, a young woman with self-doubts who was unsure of herself. A woman who was very terrified of a now dead man.

Would Carmen have confronted Darius in a fit of rage? Fed up that he would come back into her life and try to destroy her future with Cedric.

Carmen answered the second time I tried to call her. "Hello, Ms. Eugeena. Did you find Cedric?"

"I did. He was sleeping at the hospital. He's right here. Let me give him my phone."

Cedric nodded his gratitude. "Just place her on speaker phone, Mom."

Like I knew how to do that.

I will admit I've learned a lot of technology the past few years, but some of it was beyond me. I fiddled with the button that had the speaker. "Carmen, are you there?"

"Yes, I'm here. Cedric?"

"Honey, I'm here. Where are you?"

"I'm at the Charleston Place hotel."

Cedric raised his eyebrows. "Why are you there?"

"I went to see Darius this morning. I wanted to tell him he had to leave me alone. It was too late though."

"What do you mean?" I asked. "Was his hotel door open? Did you see anyone else around him?" My amateur detective hat was officially on.

"The door was slightly open, and no, I didn't see anyone. I just pushed the door open and walked in. He was lying on the floor staring up at the ceiling. There was blood underneath him around the back of his head. I ran out, but I knew I needed to call the police. So, I did and waited for them in the lobby."

"Oh, poor Carmen." I said. "We're coming to get you."

"No, Cedric shouldn't come here."

He frowned. "Why not? I have nothing to hide, Carmen. I didn't even know the guy, nor did I know anything about him being at that hotel. I'm coming to get you right now."

"There's no need. I already gave them my statement. I'll meet you at home so we can talk."

Carmen ended the call, leaving us in silence. I placed the phone back in my purse. "What are you going to do?"

Cedric shrugged his shoulders.

"Amos is outside. He's making some calls. Maybe he can get some more information for us."

"I'm going to let Maddy know I'll be out for a bit." He shook his head. "I wish I hadn't left last night. I didn't know what else to do. It was all a shock. You know I love Carmen. I just couldn't understand why she'd keep this from me. I mean if this guy hadn't showed up, would she have ever told me about him?"

"What I want to know is why did he show up and why now?" I held up my finger. "And who else would want him dead?"

Cedric stared at me, and I could see even more worry lines sketch across his face. "Mom, I know you have had a few incidents in the past year or so, but you're not going to play detective here."

"I was just thinking aloud. Don't tell me that you

wouldn't want to know the same thing. They could be looking at Carmen as a suspect. Suppose they question you?" I stepped back. "Then, how are you both supposed to get married and have your happily ever after?"

"No one has a happily ever after. The wedding is the least of our concerns right now, Mom. Promise me you'll stay out of trouble."

I nodded and followed Cedric out of the room towards the nurse's station.

I waited as he talked to Nurse Maddy, thinking there was no way I could make any promises not to stick my nose into Darius Randall's life. If he was mean to Carmen and called himself trying to get back into her life, then he had probably done the same thing to someone else.

Who else hated Darius Randall enough to kill him? I prayed there was someone else and Carmen had not become a murderer overnight.

Chapter 5

Amos tried to follow Cedric back to the neighborhood as best as he could, but Cedric was driving at breakneck speed down I-26, mainly in the left lane. "I don't blame him for being in a hurry, but he shouldn't attract attention to himself," Amos said when we lost sight of him.

I nodded, thinking the same thing and prayed the Lord would keep my son safe. I knew he was panicked and worried about Carmen.

By the time we arrived at the home Cedric had lived in for the past ten years, it appeared as though Cedric swung his BMW into the driveway and barely cut the engine before he scrambled out. Carmen's Murano was parked carefully next to it.

Amos pulled in behind Carmen's car. Before I got out, Amos asked, "Are you sure we shouldn't give them some space?"

For a moment, Amos's question hung in the air. "I just want to make sure Carmen is okay. Then, we can go."

I really did want to know how she was holding up. I believed she hadn't done anything to that man, especially

after seeing how terrified she was yesterday. Still, it was for that very reason I wanted to hear for myself why Carmen purposely sought the man out.

Alone.

Anyone who watched enough horror movies or any *Lifetime* movie about crazy exes knew you just don't confront the person alone, and I knew Carmen secretly liked watching those movies even though she complained about the stupid plots.

I walked up to the door and started to ring the doorbell when Amos tapped me on the shoulder. "We may want to come back later, Eugeena. Looks like Cedric and Carmen have company." He tilted his head to the left to indicate someone was behind us.

I turned around to see a familiar looking Crown Victoria pull up in front of the house. The driver seemed small in the front seat, but I knew from past experience the petite woman who climbed out of the car was a tough cookie.

Detective Sarah Wilkes walked around the car towards the house. She was dressed in her usual uniform of khaki pants and a white shirt. Her official badge hung from her neck. She approached, and I noticed her freckled face appeared grim as she stared in our direction.

"Mrs. Patterson and Mr. Jones, why am I not surprised to see you both here?"

"Well, we're here to check on Carmen," I offered.

Amos added, "I understand you already took her statement."

Wilkes' red hair was much longer now than when I first met her, but she kept it in her standard ponytail which hung down her back. "I'm here to speak to Dr. Cedric

Patterson." Her right eyebrow raised as she glanced at me. "From my memory, he's your son."

"Yes, he is, and you won't find out anything from him."

Detective Wilkes smirked. "I will be the judge of that, Mrs. Patterson."

At that moment the front door opened, and we all peered through the screen door as Carmen looked out at us. Her red-rimmed eyes passed over me and Amos, finally resting on Detective Wilkes. Her shoulders heaved as if she let out a huge sigh before opening the door. "Did you need something else, Detective Wilkes?"

"I need to talk to your fiancé."

Carmen's eyes grew wide. "Why?"

Cedric's voice floated from behind her. "It's okay, Carmen. Let's get this over with."

Carmen stepped to the side, eyeing Detective Wilkes as if she was the enemy. I followed with Amos close behind. I stepped beside Carmen and reached up to rub her shoulder. "How are you holding up?"

She shook her head and whispered before closing the door and heading to the living room. "Not too good. This has become a nightmare." Amos stood off to the side near the dining room area and I joined him to stay out of Detective Wilkes' way.

Cedric caught my eye, but then looked away as Detective Wilkes sat on the chair opposite where he and Carmen sat together on the couch. I couldn't help but notice there was significant space between Cedric and his bride-to-be. Not afraid of public affection, I've seen these two practically glued together even in my own house. It pained me to see the gap and I hoped it wouldn't get much worse.

Detective Wilkes began. "Dr. Patterson, please tell me

your whereabouts between the hours of 12:00 a.m. and 7:00 a.m.?"

That time frame had to be when Darius was killed. My love of detective television shows taught me that much.

Cedric stared back at Detective Wilkes. "I'm not sure precisely when I arrived at the hospital, but I'm fairly certain when I checked in with nurses on duty it was after midnight."

"What were you doing prior to checking in?"

"I drove around for a bit, then I drove to the hospital and sat in the car for a while. I came in, spoke to the security officer and then checked on my patients. I talked to the nurses on duty and grabbed some sleep. I woke this morning to my mom saying Carmen was looking for me."

Detective Wilkes was jotting down notes and remained quiet for what seemed like a long time. She peered up at Cedric, "You said you spoke to the security guard, so he was the first person to notice you in the hospital?"

Cedric shrugged. "Yes, that would be correct."

"You don't recall noting the time until you talked to the night shift nurses?"

"There's a big clock that hangs behind the nurses' station. I want to say it was after midnight. I could be wrong."

"But you spoke to the nurses on duty?"

"Like I said, I checked in with them."

Detective Wilkes stared at him, "So how long would you say you visited with your patients?"

"About fifteen or twenty minutes. They were asleep, so I checked their charts and stepped back out of the room."

Wilkes shifted her gaze to Carmen and back to Cedric. "I understand you and Ms. Alpine had an argument last night. What time did you leave?"

Cedric frowned. "I don't know. I was too upset to notice."

"So you just drove around town for a few hours before arriving at the hospital?"

Cedric nodded.

Wilkes continued. "You didn't happen to drive by the Charleston Place Hotel?"

"Not that I remember." Cedric answered back with a sharp tone to his voice. "I'd like to remind you because I see where you're going with your questions, I've never met Darius Randall in my life. I wouldn't even know what he looked like, and I only learned about him last night. I certainly wouldn't have had time to track him down."

"But Ms. Alpine had Mr. Randall's information. You could have found it."

Cedric whipped around to look at Carmen.

The look my son gave Carmen stabbed me in my heart. I'd seen Cedric hurt before, but this expression hovered between unbelief and pain.

Carmen returned Cedric's gaze before turning away. Her voice was so low, I had to lean forward to hear her. "I saw Darius briefly at the hospital when I was visiting a patient. I was surprised, shocked really. Anyway, before I could walk away, he gave me a business card. He wrote his hotel information on the back before he handed it to me."

Cedric's tone was sharp. "His hotel room number. Really? You stood there long enough for him to write down his hotel information?"

"It's been almost ten years," Carmen said, "I don't know why he did that or what he wanted."

Cedric stood. "Why did you go over there?"

Detective Wilkes held up her hand. "Dr. Patterson,

please. You can discuss this with your fiancée later. I haven't finished your statement."

Cedric glared. "I have nothing else to say. I don't exactly go through Carmen's things. After we argued, I left. If you have other questions for me, then I will need to get a lawyer." He jabbed his fingers at her. "You can't place me near a crime scene."

With that, Cedric walked out.

I started to go after him, but Amos stopped me. "Let me do this, man to man. Somebody needs to keep an eye on Carmen. That girl might fall apart."

I looked back at Carmen who had tears streaming down her face. I nodded to Amos and watched as he darted out after Cedric. I walked over to the couch and placed my hand on Carmen's shoulder. "Do we need to continue this now, Detective Wilkes?"

The detective stared at Carmen and then looked over at me. "I will reach out to Dr. Alpine or Dr. Patterson if I need to."

"I didn't do anything," Carmen wailed. "I just went over there this morning to ask him to leave me alone. He's done enough to me in the past."

"Shhhh," I encouraged Carmen. "We know you didn't do anything." Something Carmen said earlier struck me at that moment. "You said Darius had been here since last week."

Carmen nodded. "Yes, I saw him Thursday."

"The Charleston Place Hotel is pretty expensive. For him to stay a whole week would have cost a fortune. What did he do for a living, Carmen?" I asked.

She shook her head. "I don't know. He was an accountant when we were married. He had a large salary and always liked nice things."

I looked over at Detective Wilkes who was watching us with interest. "Do you know what he did, Detective Wilkes? Sounds like he was, as the young kids say, a baller."

Detective Wilkes raised her eyebrows. "And why do you find this interesting, Mrs. Patterson?"

I smiled back at the detective knowing she didn't want me poking my nose in her case, but still unable to resist. "Because, Detective, as you probably already know, money is the root of all evil."

The detective returned my smile with her own wry smile. "I'm betting that Mr. Randall's death was one of passion. I doubt money had anything to do with it." She turned to Carmen, "I will be in touch, Dr. Alpine."

I got up to walk the detective out. From the window outside, I could see Amos talking to Cedric on the porch. Both men turned as Detective Wilkes walked out towards her car. I hoped Amos had talked some sense into Cedric's head. He really didn't need to lose his temper in front of the detective that way.

I had a feeling Detective Wilkes' was focusing on Carmen for the murder. She found the man and had a pretty good motive, but I also sensed the detective was missing some vital details and I intended to find those out.

As soon as I saw the detective drive off, I stepped outside. "Both of you get in here now. We have work to do."

My son and Amos looked at me, their eyes wide like a deer staring into oncoming headlights. I hissed at them both. "Move it. We've got to get to the bottom of this now. Detective Wilkes already has her suspect in mind."

I turned and went back into the house. This woman in front of me with the tear-stained face was supposed to become my future daughter-in-law. In all honesty, I should be spitting mad with her for keeping such a huge secret. And for crying out loud, why go see the man?

I'd learned in the past few years that Carmen was a genuinely good woman, and I had been spending too much time the last few months planning a wedding. I didn't particularly like spending my free time in vain. Nothing was going to stop me, not even a murderer.

Chapter 6

I sat next to Carmen on the couch and looked up to see Cedric and Amos slowly enter the room. "Sit," I commanded. I reached out and touched Carmen's arm. "Carmen, you need to tell us the whole story or instead of walking down the aisle, you may be sitting in a jail cell in a few weeks. I'm not about to let that happen, you hear me."

Carmen's eyes threatened to spill more tears. She looked over at Cedric.

I followed her gaze and examined my son, who for a few seconds looked ready to bolt. The disappointment in his eyes made me catch my own breath. Cedric was the one who never seemed to get along with his father, Ralph Patterson. He also was the one who looked so much like his father. I'd witnessed that wary look and staunch silence in Ralph so many times. Dear man had been gone five years and I'd almost forgotten this look. Here it was glaring sullenly back at Carmen.

I watched as Cedric's chest rose as if he was sighing deeply, preparing himself for the rest of the truth his fiancée would deliver. He sank down on the other half of the sectional couch that dominated the living room. The soft, black leather couch was left over from Cedric's bachelor days. I knew it was the one sore spot in the living room that Carmen looked forward to getting rid of when she became Mrs. Cedric Patterson. The *if* word hung in the air ready to crash to the floor in a million pieces.

I glanced over at Amos who'd scooted back towards the dining area, opting to pull out a chair away from the center of my family drama. I felt bad for including him, but I needed him. Not just for his old detective skills. I wasn't sure if I was prepared myself for what Carmen would tell us.

Carmen clasped her hands in her lap and sat with her shoulders hunched as if she was expecting one of us to throw something at her at any moment.

I encouraged again. "Carmen, we're almost family. We want to help you. It's no doubt in my mind that Detective Wilkes will come back and haunt you about this man's death. She looks like she wants to accuse you, and she wasn't that convinced about Cedric's whereabouts either. It worries me that she's going to focus on y'all and not look for the real killer."

Carmen shook her head. "He was already dead. I called the police. If I had killed him, why would I call them? I could have just walked away."

That's true. I rubbed my hands down my arms as if I had caught a chill. It didn't matter what I thought, we needed proof that someone else had it out for this man. "Well, I'm not sure if the detective will see it that way. Tell us everything, starting from when Darius first contacted you last week."

Carmen glanced at Cedric once more before starting. "Last Thursday, I'd seen patients all day and was on an extra-long shift at the hospital since I had a patient with some complications. I walked off the elevator and saw Darius Randall walking towards me. It took him a few seconds to recognize me. My hair is different. I wore it longer, straight and it was darker. But then I saw the recognition in his eyes. I probably should have walked by faster, held my head down or something."

I urged Carmen to continue. "You seemed practically terrified of him yesterday."

"When I ran into him at the hospital, it was so weird." She squeezed her hands as though she was wringing out a dishcloth. "He claimed he was in town visiting someone, but he never said who. He didn't mention anything about me getting married during that conversation. It was like he just saw me and wanted to ask how I was doing."

"So, was he stalking you?" Cedric's voice was strained as if trying to control his anger. "Why didn't you say something before now? We could have reported him to the police before all of this."

Carmen shook her head. "With what, Cedric? I couldn't go to the police and say I ran into the man who made my life hell almost ten years ago." She wrapped her arms around her as if shielding herself.

"I didn't know to be scared until he showed up at the bakery yesterday morning. I panicked because Ms. Eugeena was there. I don't know. I saw something in his eyes. Desperation, maybe? I just wanted us to get out of there, Ms. Eugeena."

I thought for a minute. "Are you sure you're telling us everything? You seemed preoccupied the entire time we were in the bakery."

Carmen shook her head and briefly closed her eyes. She snapped them open and stared at nothing in particular on the coffee table. "Darius called yesterday morning. He wanted to see me over a cup of coffee. I couldn't figure out how he'd gotten my cell number. I was also trying to figure out how to tell Cedric that Darius was in town attempting to see me whether I wanted to or not. Him calling out of the blue for coffee like we were old friends freaked me out. It started to dawn on me that he wasn't going away."

Carmen's voice rose as in panic at the thought. She sounded scared and desperate. I hoped Carmen hadn't appeared the same way to the detective.

Desperate people did dangerous things.

I decided to change the direction of the conversation. "You said he came in from out of town. Where was he living?"

She shook her head. "When we were married, we lived in Charlotte. I graduated from Northwestern High School in Rock Hill, which isn't that far from Charlotte. Darius always talked about moving to Atlanta. I assumed he moved there after our divorce. Of course, I didn't keep up with him. My parents settled in Asheville about five years ago. I've never run into Darius until last week."

I was reaching for information, not sure what I was looking for Carmen to tell us. It wasn't like I was a professional detective.

"You said he was an accountant?" I asked, still curious about the man's wealth, "He must have been paid really well to be able to stay at a fancy place like the Charleston Place Hotel." I had a high school friend who was a staff manager at that place. I made a note in my head to reach out to her later.

Carmen acknowledged. "Darius kept the books for some pretty large firms. He may have moved on to bigger things. Back then, he owned a Jaguar and the house we lived in was located in a gated community. He'd owned the home for several years before we were married."

"He was much older than you?"

"I was seventeen when we started dating, and he was in his late twenties. My parents didn't know until later. When I realized I was pregnant, I was already eighteen... We married a few months later."

I crossed my arms. "That's not good for a man to marry a woman so young. I know your parents were awfully upset."

It occurred to me as I said this that I thought Carmen was awfully young for Cedric when I first met her. Now Carmen was twenty-eight and Cedric was turning forty in a few months. Despite an eleven year difference I no longer felt the age gap was odd. I turned my attention back to Carmen as she shared her story.

She took a deep breath. "My parents warned me not to consider marrying him. They said they would help me with the baby, but I wanted to have a family. I was adopted, and I wanted my own child to be raised in a real family. His or her own family. I was so naive at the time. I didn't realize what a control freak Darius was. His temper was terrifying. He was an awful man."

"There had to be other people he turned that temper on. The wrong person. Probably the one who killed him." I patted Carmen on the hand. "What prompted you to meet with him today?"

Carmen eyed Cedric for a few seconds. "I was talking to Jocelyn last night after Cedric left. She suggested I face him, tell him to go away and stop bothering me."

I raised my eyebrow. "Jocelyn told you that?"

A year ago, Jocelyn Miller, Carmen's BFF, had been mired in her own legal trouble. In the midst of it, she'd sought out and found her maternal grandmother. Now the young woman lived with Louise Hopkins, who'd been my next-door neighbor for almost thirty years. I would be visiting with them tonight. Seemed like pretty bad advice to me.

"Did Jocelyn say anything to Darius about the wedding?" I asked.

Carmen shook her head. "No, she never talked to Darius. In fact, when I was seeing him, Jocelyn warned me something wasn't right about him. I remember getting mad at her and accusing her of being jealous. She wasn't, of course. She just saw what I couldn't. That he was a real creep."

"How many people knew about your marriage?" I asked.

"Not that many people." Carmen seemed lost in her recollections before speaking. "We were married at a small chapel in Asheville. I'm still not sure who arranged it all. Jocelyn was there. My parents. No one was there with Darius."

My own wedding was a small affair, not in our family church either. When I got pregnant with Junior, my older brother, my then surrogate father paid a visit to Ralph Patterson. I was pretty sure my brother was, as the young folks say, "packin." Next thing I knew, a few months later, I was married. My story wasn't too different from Carmen's.

I did think it odd that Carmen mentioned Darius was alone. "He didn't have any family or friends?"

Carmen took in a breath. "Not at the chapel. Later, before I lost the baby, I'd met a few of his acquaintances. They were all kind of like him. Wealthy, liked to spend money. They didn't seem real. I remember feeling awkward."

I thought about the current wedding we were planning.

I knew Carmen had asked Jocelyn to be her maid of honor. My daughter, Leesa was one of the bridesmaids. Cedric had asked his brother, Junior, to be his best man and one of his friends from college, Larry Holmes, to be a groomsman. Larry lived in Charlotte. I pondered aloud, "I mailed the invitations Monday. There were seventy-five of them, and he certainly wasn't on the list."

Carmen frowned. "No, absolutely not!" She blew out a breath as if to clear her system of any mention of Darius. Suddenly sitting up straight, Carmen uttered, "Wait. Leesa set up a website on eWedding.com. I don't know. Maybe if someone was searching for my name, they might find the website."

That's true. I did searches all the time. I had even searched for a few old classmates I lost contact with. I also thought about other places I searched. "Are you posting the wedding plans on Facebook?"

Carmen's eyes grew wide. "I don't have time to post much, but yes, I posted a few photos on Instagram, and then sent them to my Facebook page."

"So it's possible if someone was looking for you, you know trying to see what you've been up to all these years, they could find out from your Facebook page?" I asked.

Carmen nodded. "Yes, I changed my status to engaged to Cedric Patterson. I even posted a photo of the engagement ring awhile back, and there are a few photos of Cedric and me." She turned towards Cedric. "I tagged Cedric in those photos."

Cedric's eyes were focused in our direction. "I'm not on Facebook that often either, but I read all the comments on the engagement ring. I have the same status. Engaged to Carmen Alpine."

After Cedric's statement, I stood and turned my eyes

towards Amos. He gazed back at me, concern in his eyes. I smiled, grateful he was here. I needed to move around. As if movement would make sense of the two lovebirds in front of me whose lives had been shattered by Carmen's discovery this morning.

Yes, we had established some possibilities of how Darius Randall could have found out about the upcoming wedding. But it didn't help the bride-to-be who was now a possible murder suspect. If anything, we'd confirmed Carmen had a perfectly good reason to kill Darius.

I paced the floor, knowing it was time to go deeper into Carmen's reasoning. "This morning you went over to the hotel. I assume you already had the room number from the business card. Did you call ahead of time? Did he know you were coming?"

"No, he didn't know I was coming."

"That's good." I looked at Amos. "There's been no contact from Carmen to Darius on his phone.

Amos nodded. "Yes, but it can work against Carmen. She also just showed up and her reasons definitely interested Detective Wilkes."

I eyed Amos. "You're not helping."

The eyes of a retired cop gazed back. Soon, his eyes began to soften. "I'm sorry, Eugeena. You're right, the police would need to get Mr. Randall's phone and find out who else he'd been corresponding with the past few days. The inquiry could lead to other suspects."

I sighed. "Good. That's the direction we need Detective Wilkes to take." Still, I knew Amos was right. "Carmen, you found the body. There has to be something else you noticed."

Carmen glanced over at Cedric who sat looking off into space as if he wanted to be anywhere, but here. "When I arrived, I parked my car towards the back. The parking lot was pretty filled up. I took the elevator up to his room."

"Which floor?" I interrupted.

"It was the eighth floor. Room 828."

Amos stepped closer into the living room. "Did you notice anyone coming off the elevator or in the hallway? From my understanding, Darius was hit from behind."

I gasped. "So, he knew the person he let into the room. As soon as he turned his back, he or she hit him over the head. With what though?"

Amos answered. "From what I can gather from an old friend on the force, he was hit from behind with an object, but it wasn't found at the scene."

I frowned. "So the killer took the weapon with them?"

Carmen stretched out her hands. "Well, I don't have anything like that on me."

Amos eyed her. "Still, the detective may want to come back and search your car and the house. I wouldn't be surprised if Detective Wilkes was securing search warrants now."

Cedric looked up, the fire back into his eyes. "So what should we do?"

Amos sighed. "Now may be the time to start calling a lawyer or lawyers. You will both probably want separate lawyers."

"Lawyers!" I squealed. "They haven't done anything. Won't having lawyers make them look guilty?"

Amos looked around the room. "Better to be prepared for whatever is coming."

At that moment, a piercing noise radiated the room. Both Cedric and Carmen peered down at their phones.

Cedric frowned, and then a sense of relief crossed his face. He rose from the seat. "I need to head back to the hospital. My patient needs me." He looked at Carmen. "We'll talk about all this later." Cedric grabbed his keys from the table by the front door and left.

I didn't know if it was a good idea to leave Carmen alone. "Have you reached out to your family?"

Carmen nodded. "I talked to my mom last night, but I haven't told her what happened this morning. My parents are going to freak out. They would not have approved of me seeing Darius this morning. I almost wished I hadn't, but I had to face him sometime. Funny, I didn't need to... Someone else took care of it."

"They left with the murder weapon too. I wonder what it was." I turned to Amos. "How can you smack someone in the head and just walk out the hotel with the murder weapon?"

Amos shrugged. "The weapon could have been discarded in the hotel."

It felt past lunch time. "Carmen, I know you've had a difficult week with this man showing back up in your life. Do you need anything?"

She shook her head. "No. I just wished Darius had never tried to contact me. What was his point? I hadn't heard from him in almost ten years."

Those were my exact thoughts. "You hadn't heard anything about him getting married again? It would seem odd for him to spend all this time alone."

Carmen sank back into the seat. "I don't know if he remarried, but I'm sure Darius had plenty of women. The brief time I was married to him, I also realized too late that he was a ladies' man. He had no qualms with flirting with other women and I'm sure picking them up, even when he was married to me."

We needed to find out more about Darius Randall. I

was still suspicious about the man's finances. He obviously liked to live a life of luxury and seemed to not have a problem with getting women. Still, how did he find out about Carmen and her pending nuptials? Why did he want to reach out to Carmen after all these years? Surely the man had moved on by now.

There were so many questions for me and I had all the time in the world to find the answers.

Chapter 7

Amos and I left Cedric and Carmen's home. I wasn't sure what Cedric was thinking, but I could only hope he would have a reasonable conversation with Carmen and not do anything rash. I probably should be a lot more upset with Carmen, but I'd grown fond of her. I wanted to see their relationship survive. Besides, after the wedding ceremony is when the real marriage trials started. If those two could make it through this ordeal, they were pretty solid for the death do us part vows to come.

I climbed into the car, and Amos said, "I know that didn't satisfy your curiosity. What are your plans now?"

"There has to be somebody else who wanted the man dead. I have a friend who is a manager at the Charleston Place Hotel. Maybe we can ask her some questions."

Amos frowned. "We? What kind of questions? People come in and out of the hotel all the time. The staff doesn't always pay attention."

Recalling stories Rosemary Gladstone had shared with me, I wasn't ready to agree with Amos. I still thought that should be the first place to start.

"Don't worry. I won't do anything crazy. I'm just going to talk to my friend, Rosemary. She knows everything that goes on in that place."

Amos gave me a look like he wasn't sure whether he believed me. He started the car and backed out of the driveway.

For some reason, the mention of Rosemary's name triggered another thought in my mind. I pulled out my phone and noticed I was supposed to have the church open by now for the children arriving off the bus.

Where had the time gone?

My mind spun into a panic. I usually volunteered every weekday for the program, and I'd already taken Tuesday off to help Carmen with wedding errands.

At the rate I was going, I would need to call for backup. I dreaded doing so because that meant I had to call the Brown sisters. Annie Mae and Willie Mae Brown. I attended Missionary Baptist Church and served on the usher board with the twins. They also lived in my neighborhood, so we've known each other a long time.

Some days, they were too much for one person to handle, both individually and definitely together.

Last year, I received approval from Pastor Reverend George Jones to write the grant for the afterschool program. When we received the funding and parents started signing up their children, I soon realized I would need volunteers. Of course, fellow retirees, Willie Mae and Annie Mae signed up. I couldn't exactly tell them no because I needed the help. They were a bit more stern with the children than me, but in this day and age, discipline was needed.

We ran a tight ship, but today I slipped way off my responsibilities. As soon as Amos drove up to my house,

I hopped out of the car and leaned over before closing the door. "I've been so distracted, I forgot about the afterschool program. I need to call some backup so I can get to the hotel."

He leaned towards me. "Eugeena, you should see what the police turn up before we start sticking our noses into the investigation. Detective Wilkes will figure out the truth."

"I'm sorry, but I don't agree with you. I saw the look in that detective's eyes." I sighed deeply before a smile took over my face. I peered at Amos. "You do know I appreciate you, right?"

He winked. "I know. Just promise me you will stay out of trouble. If you need me, you know how to find me."

I winked back. "I'll do my best." I closed the car door and watched Amos back out of my driveway. As I opened the door to my home, I knew my best may not be good enough. I had too many nagging questions on my mind.

First, I needed to take care of a few necessities.

Porgy hopped off the doggy bed next to the couch and raced from the corner of the living room. He followed me around towards the kitchen where I let him out the back door. I'd neglected the poor dog, and he raced around the backyard as if experiencing freedom for the first time.

While I kept an eye on the dog, I reached into my pocketbook and pulled out my phone to call the twins.

On the second ring, Annie Mae, the eldest of the twins answered. I recognized her raspy voice, a reflection of her past love of tobacco. "Hello?"

"Hello, Annie Mae. This is Eugeena. I hate to ask, but can you or Willie Mae open the church? Something has come up and I will not be able to make the afterschool program today."

"What? This is your baby, Eugeena. What's going on that you can't be there for the children today?"

I took a brief glance at my phone. It was almost three o'clock, and the bus would be arriving any minute. "Family emergency. Please, just this once. I will be there for the rest of the week."

"Everything alright with Leesa? Are her children sick?"

"They're fine. I'll explain everything soon, right now I need someone to open the church. Today was you or Willie Mae's turn to volunteer, right?"

I could hear Annie Mae talking in the background before she addressed me. She returned to the phone. "Willie Mae is on her way. She was already dressed and ready to go. I can go with her so she has some help."

Shock almost made me forget to speak. I was expecting the twins to give me a lot more fuss. "Thank you both so much. I appreciate it."

I got off the phone and immediately felt bad. One, because I'd have to come up with something to tell the Brown sisters. They weren't going to let me off scot free. Then again, I had noticed a change in the twins this past year. A lot of tragedy hit Sugar Creek in recent years, including the loss of Willie Mae's daughter, Pat Brown. I still felt as though I'd lost a member of my own family. I knew deep down the sisters volunteered for the program because they knew it was something Pat would've done if she were still alive.

Still, there was no way I was telling the Brown sisters that my future daughter-in-law found her ex-husband dead. It pained me that I would miss the children today from the afterschool program. I'd taught social studies in the Charleston School District for most of my teaching career. It wasn't an easy job, especially the last decade or so. Most children were flat out not interested in history, and I knew in my heart, the history we had to teach to meet the standards didn't always tell the whole story. I smiled because I would especially miss talking to Amani Gladstone who had become one of my favorites. She was a sharp nine-year-old with a love for history.

I called to Porgy who'd become consumed with chasing a squirrel. "Alright, boy, that's enough outside time. Come on in." It took me a few more tries which resulted in me going out and chasing the dog into the house. What a scene that must have been for someone to see, dog chasing squirrel, and a slightly overweight, old woman chasing a dog. It took me a moment to catch my breath. I wasn't going to complain too much at my four-legged adopted child because I needed the exercise.

After washing my hands, I hunted around my kitchen for something to eat and decided on a quick soup and salad. I needed to do something with the lettuce since it always went bad first. I opted for some chicken soup I had in the freezer. I popped the bowl into the microwave and checked my phone for Rosemary Gladstone's number. I had it listed since she was one of Amani's emergency contacts in case her mother, a nurse, was not available. I needed to visit with Amani's maternal grandmother at the Charleston Place Hotel. It seemed important to visit while the topic of murder had to be fresh on her mind.

A young woman answered my call. "Hello, Charleston Place Hotel."

I guessed she must be Rosemary's administrative assistant. "Yes, I'm calling for Mrs. Gladstone. Is she available?"

"She's in a meeting right now. Can I take a message for her?"

I glanced at the apple shaped clock on my kitchen wall. "Do you know how much longer she will be in the meeting?" I knew Rosemary usually stuck around the hotel until after five o'clock. She'd come to pick up Amani a few times from the church.

"I'm not really sure, she's been in there with the police for some time."

"The police?"

"Oh, I mean...well, she's in a meeting. Nothing bad. How about I take a message?"

"No, thanks. I will check in later." I ended the call thinking Rosemary had a bit of a blabber mouth for an assistant. I was sure the woman didn't mean to let it slip about the police meeting with her boss. The woman was probably shaken up about the events that occurred at the hotel today. Everyone on staff would know and be horrified. From my recollection, nothing like this had ever happened at the hotel, at least not to my knowledge. I wondered if it would be on the local news. As long as Carmen wasn't mentioned... One could only hope!

I grabbed the soup out of the microwave and finished assembling my salad with cherry tomatoes, cucumbers and my absolute favorite topping, shredded cheese. I topped the salad off with a low-fat ranch dressing, a taste I was still learning to adapt to.

As I consumed my lunch, I prepared questions in my mind. The more questions I thought about, the more I tried to talk myself out of going. Then, I remembered my daughter Leesa had the Charleston Place Hotel on her list of places for the reception. I hadn't talked to my other children yet and didn't know if Cedric had confided in them. Knowing Cedric, his attention was probably on his patients. That would be his way of handling the situation.

It's why last night after driving around he ended up at the hospital instead of returning home.

I wondered if Carmen would have not considered going to the hotel this morning if he'd returned home. None of us could change the past, but I planned to do something about the future.

I speed dialed my daughter's cell knowing she would still be at work. Leesa had recently started a job as an administrative assistant for an insurance company, and I was really proud of her. I knew she'd grown tired and worn out from the minimum wage retail jobs. Now she had a real nine-to-five that helped support her two children, Keisha and Tyric. At one time, I was watching them for her, but then Leesa finally started collecting child support from Tyric's dad which made it possible to send both children to daycare. Keisha was now in first grade.

Leesa answered. "Mom, is everything okay?"

I wasn't sure if she'd talked to her brother yet and didn't want to break anything to her. Of her two brothers, Leesa was closest to Cedric. Which is why it was no surprise when she volunteered to help her brother with his wedding.

"I'm on my way to see Rosemary at the Charleston Place Hotel. Did you settle on a location for the reception yet?"

"Actually, I was leaning towards a room at the Charleston Place, but I kind of got off track this week. I've been really busy with work."

"Busy is good. Do you want me to ask her about the rates? I know this was your thing to do."

"Yes, please ask her. I think the rooms are beautiful and Carmen's parents have a pretty good budget. Sounds like they've been looking forward to her getting married."

But she was married before. Though I would wager that

first marriage was definitely not what Carmen's parents envisioned. Their daughter marrying a respectable doctor was everything to them.

"Great. I will call you later to let you know what Rosemary said."

"Thanks, Mom. I appreciate it."

After ending the call, I was grateful Cedric hadn't shared anything with his sister. Knowing my drama queen daughter, she wouldn't react well when she did find out. She would no doubt think all her efforts towards helping Carmen plan the wedding were in vain. That meant I needed to keep progress moving in the right direction as much as possible.

It also meant I had a legitimate purpose for seeing Rosemary. I was bringing her business, and I was officially on the case. Tracking down Darius' killer.

Chapter 8

Built in 1939, the Charleston Place Hotel was a mixture of old and modern. When you stepped onto the marbled floor of the lobby, the hotel felt like old wealth. A large chandelier hung from the middle of the ceiling. It almost felt like going back in time, a time before even I was born. Despite the expensive marble and mahogany woodwork, the guest counter in front of me held touches of the twenty-first century. Three computer monitors peeked from the top of the counter.

Off to the side, I caught sight of a large flat screen television mounted on the wall in the middle of a sitting area. The furniture was elegant, but not too stuffy as to discourage guests from lounging.

I walked up to the desk where a young man dressed in a crisp white shirt and blue blazer greeted me. He had to be no older than my Leesa, mid-twenties. His eyes were a sharp blue and a faint mustache grew above his lips. He stretched his mouth wide to display perfect white teeth. "Are you checking in, ma'am?" The young man's drawl was definitely Southern but refined.

My eyes focused on his crisp reddish bow tie before grinning at him. "I'm actually looking for Rosemary Gladstone."

His smile shifted slightly. Rosemary was his boss, the hotel staff manager. "Sure, she was in meetings earlier, but I will check to see if she's available." He picked up the phone. "May I tell her who's asking for her?"

"Eugeena Patterson. I'm here about my son's wedding reception."

The man's smile brightened. "Oh, yes. We're the perfect place for a wedding reception."

The young man dialed Rosemary, and I turned my head to examine the hotel lobby more closely. Guests were bustling in and out the doors, probably to head downtown to explore the shops and restaurants nearby. A doorman wheeled two oversized rolling pieces of luggage while a lady walked alongside. A man brought up the rear, hefting a large duffel bag in his arms.

The young man behind the counter caught my attention. "Mrs. Patterson, Rosemary will be with you in a few minutes."

"Thank you." I walked away just as the woman sauntered to the counter. She appeared exuberant, a smile spread across her face. I overheard the woman say, "We're here to check-in. We're on our honeymoon."

How nice. Cedric and Carmen were quite okay with not having a big wedding. Had they even thought about the honeymoon part? Right now, I needed to make sure they made it to the wedding part.

I glanced around, people were lounging in the seating area. It certainly didn't appear to look like a crime had occurred here earlier this morning. I took a look around the hallway where I knew the elevators were located. This morning, Carmen walked in armed with Darius's room number which was on the eighth floor. Room 828. Carmen mentioned he added the info to the back of his business card. Seemed rather bizarre the more I thought about it. The man was certainly forward.

I tried not to let it bother me, but for some reason now that I was here, I felt some kind of way that Carmen would meet the man in his hotel room. She was clearly upset at the sight of him yesterday.

Was it only because I was there with her? If she was really that scared of him, why meet him in his hotel room?

"Eugeena, how are you?"

I turned as a woman about my size came up to me. I'd known Rosemary Gladstone since we were school girls. She hadn't changed much other than to gain weight. Instead of letting her gray hair show, Rosemary opted to color her short wavy hair honey blonde. Once a former homecoming queen as well as a beauty pageant contestant, her caramel skin still looked beautiful despite being in her sixties.

She reached over to hug me. "It's been awhile. I'm still amazed you decided to spend your retirement years continuing to work with kids. Amani talks about you all the time. Speaking of the afterschool program, hasn't that started today?"

"Yes, I have two other workers volunteering their time today. I so enjoy Amani and all the students. I don't miss getting up early in the morning to teach but hanging out with the children in the afternoon has been a blessing. We need something to keep us young."

"I know about that, most of my staff are young enough to be my grandchildren. But you're here for something really exciting. I bet you are so thrilled Cedric is getting married. Looked like he would be a bachelor for life."

"Oh, I know. Leesa is actually in charge of the reception, and she's really interested in holding it here. I'm sure the bride's parents will love the place."

"Well, let me show you the rooms we have. When is the wedding?"

I sucked in a breath. "October twenty-second. They really didn't want a big wedding, but between our families, we convinced them to include us in their nuptials. Our invitation list is around seventy-five and RSVPs are starting to come in."

Rosemary's smile wavered. "Wow! That's really short notice, Eugeena. I tell you what, let's look at the rooms. Since you came to me instead of my event planner, I will try to work something out. We've been friends too long for me not to be a part of this family event."

I clasped my hands together. "Thank you. Lead the way." I followed Rosemary, feeling a bit guilty. When the right time came, I would have to ask her questions that pertained to my other intentions.

We walked in the opposite direction of the elevators, down a long hall with tall windows that looked out onto a fountain and garden. I noticed several people crowding the hallway.

"Do you have many conferences at this hotel?"

"Oh yes, we host one to two conferences a week. Charleston has always had a string of tourists, but we have a lot of entrepreneur and business type conferences who like our hotel."

"Really, what kind of conference is going on today?"

"Hmmm, my event planner, Kathy Ross would know more, but the one that's here today seems to have a lot of financial advisors. I've had so many people come up to me and my staff asking us about investments and retirement funds. I guess they're here to drum up some business too."

I almost stopped in my tracks, questions swarming my mind. *Was this why Darius was here?*

Rosemary pulled open the doors to a room down the hall from the conference attendees. I followed behind her. "So how long do these conferences go these days? I think I went to a few when I was teaching, but they were only two or three days."

Rosemary nodded, "That's about the average length. At the most, a conference may go four or five days, but that's not always the case. This one started Monday and ends tomorrow. In fact, if you want to come back, one of the rooms I wanted to show you is not occupied after tomorrow morning. This one," Rosemary cut on the lights and swept her hands out, "has a 150-person capacity. It's one of the smaller rooms we use for receptions. As you can see, the chandeliers make it very easy to convert the room to a romantic setting."

Eugeena stepped further into the room, trying to keep her mind on the task at hand. "This is a beautiful room. Would we work with your staff for catering?"

Rosemary pulled out brochures and handed them to me. For some reason, I hadn't noticed her clipboard. A memory of Rosemary being the student council president of our class sprang to my mind. This woman had always been prepared which explained how she went from desk clerk to top management over the years.

I flipped through a brochure, taking note of the rental price. "Thank you, Rosemary. Like I said, Leesa ultimately will work out the details. I'm mainly helping Carmen with the ceremony details — the cake, her bridal party and her dress."

"Oh my, you really are busy. That's quite a bit of assistance there."

"Well, I wanted the best. Speaking of the best, we love this hotel." I dropped my voice and drew closer. "When I called earlier, someone mentioned you were meeting with the police. Is everything okay?"

Rosemary's expression went from jubilant to stressed. "Who told you that?"

Not wanting to get anyone in trouble, I said, "I don't remember who I spoke with. But you know my neighbor, Amos Jones, used to be a policeman. I think he heard something too. Did something happen this morning?" I added quickly, "I mean should we be worried about anything?"

Rosemary sighed and looked around the room as if someone was hiding in the corner. She turned and closed the door behind us. "This really doesn't have any bearing on the hotel. We do our best to provide a quality service to our guests."

I stepped in closer. "Something happened to a guest? Was the guest someone at this conference?"

She nodded. "I guess you will probably hear this on the news tonight. It's not like we can keep it quiet. Reporters have been floating in and out of here all day. Guests know something is going on, but we're not trying to scare anyone away." Rosemary held her hand to her chest as if trying to prevent an oncoming heart attack. She finally admitted, "We had a tragic incident that resulted in the loss of life this morning."

She could've just said someone was murdered. Rosemary always had an interesting spin on situations. I also knew how much she loved her job and this hotel. An incident likes this was a nightmare. I tried to show surprise on my face.

Rosemary continued, "He must have been taking a vacation here. He arrived before most others in the conference last week."

"Really? You noticed him? You have hundreds of guests."

Rosemary blew out a breath. "Well, he was hard *not* to notice. He was a very handsome guy and word gets around. He was also kind of particular. He liked his room cleaned every day and he ordered room service every morning. The same thing. Same time. The longer a guest stays, the more the staff notices them."

"That makes sense. Do the police know what happened to the guy? That must be awful for your staff to have to clean up the room. I mean was there a lot of..."

Rosemary trembled as if she felt a chill. "It was not a pretty sight. Right now, we're not allowed in the room. We have to basically order all new carpeting. It's making me crazy because it was one of our suites. Suites are very popular with businessmen who travel frequently. This guy was a world traveler, believe me. We're scrambling now to make changes since we only have a few suites."

"A suite. Sounds like a person needs to have some money. I wonder why someone would kill him."

"I don't know, but he was attending this conference. I think he may have been one of the speakers, which is probably why you may hear about him on the news." Rosemary's voice dropped to a whisper despite the fact we were the only two in a very large room. "Nothing like this has ever happened here. The conference coordinators asked us to keep it as quiet as possible, but I'm kind of worried."

I touched her arm. "Don't worry, Rosemary. Your hotel is a Charleston landmark and provides top notch service. When I walked in, I didn't notice a thing. I doubt your guests did either."

"It's quieted down now, but it was a different story this morning." Rosemary raked her hand through her hair, her eyes turned up towards the ceiling in frustration. "I can't be too upset. The cops had to do their job."

I could hear people out it the hallway. "Sounds like the conference is letting out."

Rosemary glanced at the dainty, thin gold watch on her wrist. "Yes, looks like they finished early. Maybe I can show you that room now."

Back to business for Rosemary. I wanted to ask more questions, but my idea was to see what she knew which was more than I thought. I wondered if Detective Wilkes knew the man was registered for the conference. Of course, if she was a good detective she would know.

Would the detective look into who might have been hanging out with Darius Randall? She claimed the murderer struck with passion. With a caseload of murder cases, would the detective cling to a very scared and confused Carmen as her suspect? Determined to shut and close the case.

I followed Rosemary across the hall through a swarm of suited men and women, all looking blurry eyed, probably from staring at presentations all day. I glanced back to see a young man and woman sitting at a table that probably served as the registration table.

Suppose Darius Randall's killer was here at the conference right now?

My throat tightened at the thought. The conference

ends tomorrow. That meant if Darius Randall was killed by someone here at the conference, they would be leaving tomorrow. Or could he or she have left already?

Chapter 9

Rosemary showed me the Whittington room which was considerably larger than the first room she showed me. Several guests mingled inside the large room, the layout split into four columns with several rows of royal blue chairs. A large screen with vivid words, Financial Future Conference were displayed on a greenish background that appeared to move from where we stood. My eyes were mesmerized for a moment before I realized Rosemary was speaking.

"So, this room is much larger than the Hamilton room we just left, but we have also used it for receptions. It's a great space if you want to place large round tables around the room for a dinner. The middle can be used for dancing."

"There is plenty of space, but I think the first room you showed me is more appropriate, since we want the reception to remain intimate."

Rosemary nodded. "That sounds like a plan. I will check the availability of the Hamilton room for October twenty-second. You will be working with Kathy on any catering or decorating you need done. We have a variety of layouts and menu items."

"Thank you, Rosemary. I appreciate it." I reached over and hugged her. As we walked out the room, my eyes scanned the registration table on the right. The man had walked away, but the woman remained seated behind the table.

I turned to Rosemary. "You know what? I think I'd like to check out the brochures they have on the table. You never know what else you can do to help your finances, especially on a fixed income."

Rosemary winked. "Sounds good, I plan on checking out the brochure I received earlier this week myself."

She walked away, and I sauntered in front of the table to browse.

The woman at the conference table held her head down, not paying attention to me. Her blonde hair hung across her shoulders, eyes glued to the phone in her hand. As if she grew aware of my presence, the woman lifted her head and smiled brightly. "Can I help you?"

"I just noticed your signs. Financial Future Conference. You're having a conference for financial advisors or is this for someone who is seeking financial advisement?"

The woman laughed. "Believe it or not, advisors need to keep up with the latest changes in their fields, so this is a conference for them. But I'm a local financial advisor here in Charleston if you want to talk to someone." The woman pulled out a business card and stood to reach towards me. "You can make an appointment, and I will be happy to meet with you."

I peered down at the card. Anna Hudson.

I eyed her. "Ms. Hudson, I'm an old, retired schoolteacher. Are you sure you can help me? I basically live on my retirement and my husband's pension. In a few years, I will be collecting social security. I'm a widow who volunteers her time. Maybe your advice is more for my children. One of my sons is a doctor and he's getting married to a doctor."

The woman's face brightened. "I'm sure I can help you. I'm very good at helping people stretch their dollars within their budget. I would also love to meet your son and his future wife. Is the wedding soon?"

"October twenty-second to be exact. We're thinking about this room behind you for the wedding reception."

The woman clasped her hands. "How exciting! These hotel rooms are beautiful. I can see them being decorated for a wedding reception."

I decided it was time to segue into the real reason I stopped by the table. I had no intention of considering Ms. Hudson's financial assistance. I had learned the art of being frugal quite early in my life, and managed the household finances for over forty years. Not wealthy by any means, but I was indeed blessed to not have a lot of wants. Contentment, as Paul wrote in the bible, was what I tried to practice.

I cleared my throat. "It's just a shame about this morning."

Ms. Hudson's smile wavered. "What happened this morning? I've been busy with the conference since six o'clock this morning."

"Well..." I peered around as though preparing to share a secret. Conference attendees were scattered around the hallway, but most were positioned far away from the table. I turned back to Ms. Hudson. "You may hear about this on the news, but I just heard from one of the hotel staff that someone was killed this morning."

The woman's face grew pale. "This morning? Here?"

I nodded. "Sounds like it was one of your conference attendees." I looked at the table and picked up a Financial Future Conference program. An all-American family posed outside a beautiful brick home graced the cover of the program. There was no white picket fence, but the image represented the American Dream I supposed.

I noted the text underneath the title. "Looks like your conference ends tomorrow. Is that right?" I gazed at Ms. Hudson. The woman's mouth moved, but no words spilled out.

"Are you all right, Ms. Hudson?" I looked at the business card she'd placed in my hand a few minutes before. "Anna is a pretty name. I had an aunt named Anna."

Anna's eyes were a sharp green which she focused on me. "Thank you. Uh, yes. Sure...I'm fine. It's been an exhausting week." She raised an arched eyebrow. "Do you know who was killed?"

For a split second, Darius Randall's name almost fell from my mouth, but then I thought, *would that be fair to tell this woman?* She'd just said she was exhausted. I've assisted with conferences in the past. They were a lot of work. I asked the Lord for forgiveness and said, "I'm not sure."

The woman attempted to smile, but her eyes had grown weary. "I'm sorry, of course you wouldn't know. You were asking me if I knew."

I nodded. "Anna, I'm awfully sorry for bringing bad news. I really love this hotel and I hate this happened here. We're still planning to have the wedding reception here though. It's not the hotel's fault. I mean they have no idea the kind of guests that check-in. It's not like they do background checks. They're in the business of making money."

Anna let out a strange laugh. "No, you're right. It's a business. Please, do reach out to me about helping you with your finances. I'm sure I have openings early next week."

I was just about to say thank you to Anna when I noticed her gaze move to someone else.

Someone I knew from the past.

I tilted my head down, opening the confiscated conference program. I pretended interest by flipping a page, while my ears tuned into a familiar voice. One whose nasal sharp Southern tone had not graced my ears in several years.

"Anna, are you sure you haven't seen Darius? He hasn't called me back yet. I know he was mad with me, but he didn't return my call yesterday or today."

My brain felt as if I had just sucked on an ice-cold chocolate milk shake.

She knew Darius Randall?

I hadn't seen Monique Sanders in at least five years.

In the past, she wore almost waist long hair, courtesy of some Indian woman. Today, it was a slightly different color, with auburn highlights and swept back into a swinging ponytail. When my son first introduced us during a Thanksgiving dinner, she seemed nice enough. Though, I thought her a bit standoffish. Despite the holidays and being my son's date, she chose to be on her phone rather than participate in the conversations around her.

Now here she was asking about Darius Randall.

The only other woman my Cedric had considering marrying.

He'd just considered it. Praise the Lord!

I remembered the night he stopped by the house to ask my opinion. Ralph was still alive then. He'd sat in the living room listening, but not offering any advice.

Cedric was not one to ask anyone's opinion, definitely not his Mama. But Monique had been itching to become Mrs. Cedric Patterson. Then, almost thirty-five years old, Cedric's bachelorhood began to bother him.

Really, it was more like this woman's intense pressure to walk down the aisle had made Cedric nervous. He'd told me he didn't see himself being married to Monique.

While I'd only seen the woman a few times, I immediately judged Monique as being a potential bridezilla and a daughter-in-law I was not trying to have in my family.

I told him flat out don't even bother looking for a ring. *Just let her go!*

Ralph, who usually remained quiet, spoke. "Son, listen to your Mama. Dodge that bullet."

I tried to regain my composure over this unexpected shock so I could listen to the conversation.

Anna stuttered a response to Monique. "You really shouldn't worry. You know how he can be. Maybe he went back to Atlanta already. He's a busy man. I almost thought he was going to cancel being the keynote. He was so hard to book."

Monique's voice rose. "He wouldn't leave without telling me. Besides, he came here to support me. He knows I need him now more than ever. I just don't understand why he got mad with me Monday night. I only told the truth."

I sensed a desperation in Monique's voice, almost as if she was on the verge of tears.

I saw Anna glance at me before she reached out to grab Monique's arm. I thought for a moment she was going to shake Monique. Anna's eyes were angry as she bent close.

I strained to hear what she was saying to Monique.

"I'm really sorry Darius is doing this to you. Did you think maybe he didn't want you to blurt that out to everyone yet? Look, I've been at this table most of the day. Let me go up to my room and freshen up. We can get some dinner. The bar is offering free drinks for conference attendees. Wait for me in the lobby, I'll be down in thirty minutes."

Anna grabbed a large, chic brown handbag from under the table and strode off. From the corner of my eye, I watched Monique move around the table to lean against the wall. Her attention was focused on the window opposite the wall. Outside the window, vehicles moved in and out of the parking lot, while the late afternoon sun set high in the sky.

I wasn't sure if I should be the one to break the news to Monique or not, but she was going to find out sooner or later. If she was involved with Darius, the man had given her the silent treatment. That didn't seem like much support. I walked over to the woman who could have been my daughter-in-law instead of Carmen. "Monique?"

She held a wide, glassy eyed appearance that often comes with wearing contacts, but I knew it was worry not her optical choices that caused the despair in her eyes. A slight hint of red around the rims of her eyes indicated she had been crying earlier.

"I don't know if you remember me," I continued.

"Mrs. Patterson. Cedric's mom," she said sharply as if I was the last person she wanted to see.

I stepped back as if she'd slapped me with her words. "Yes."

Her eyes pierced me, leaving me speechless for a few seconds before I found my voice. "I'm sorry for asking, but are you all right?"

Tears pooled in the corner of her eyes but didn't fall. She spoke hoarsely, "I saw Cedric's getting married."

I wasn't expecting her to mention Cedric's upcoming nuptials, but somehow it didn't surprise me that she knew. "Yes, we're thinking of having the wedding reception here."

A faint smile crossed her face and disappeared quickly. "This is a nice place for a wedding. My college roommate had her wedding reception here. I believe it was in that room."

I turned awkwardly to where Monique's finger pointed. The first room Rosemary had shown me. "Yes, it's a lovely room." I turned back to the woman, hoping to guide the conversation in a new direction.

"How are you? It's been awhile." Five years ago, this woman was desperate to get married. I didn't mean to let my eyes search, but I found myself staring at her hands for rings. There was neither an engagement ring or wedding band.

As if she knew what I was doing, Monique shifted her hands behind her. "I'm happy for Cedric. I've been dating a man for about a year. We've become serious, but I've had to put things on hold a bit. My father, I don't know if you remember him. He got sick."

I recalled Monique's dad very well. Kendall Sanders was the president of my bank for years. He often golfed with Ralph. It was these two men who held the responsibility of matchmaking gone wrong.

Cedric had dated Monique for at least two years. Two years too long.

"Yes, I remember your dad. Is he still enjoying retirement?" Kendall had retired a year before Ralph passed away if I remembered correctly.

Monique's body stiffened. "Retirement was good for him in the beginning but not now. My dad started to go downhill about a year ago."

"Age can certainly bring issues. You know Cedric's dad passed away five years ago?" Cedric broke up with Monique only a few months before Ralph's heart attack took him from us.

"Yes, I attended the funeral," she nodded, her voice somber. "My father has stage four colon cancer."

"I'm so sorry, Monique." I recalled that Kendall was a huge man, carrying his linebacker stature into his fifties. I'd not seen the man since Ralph's funeral. "I had no idea."

Monique tossed her head, making her ponytail bounce like a horse's tail. "My dad's a proud man, a bit of a recluse these days."

She glanced at her watch, one of those Apple watches with a wide screen. "I don't live in Charleston anymore. I moved to Atlanta to take a position in the bank's regional office. In the past few weeks, I've been back to care for my dad. My boyfriend arrived in town last week."

The boyfriend she'd been looking to respond to her calls since Monday night. *The man Carmen found dead this morning.* I wasn't fond of this woman, but this kind of news I wouldn't wish on a soul.

I needed to prepare her. It was the least I could do. "Monique, I don't know if you are aware, but I was talking to the hotel manager and something happened to a guest this morning."

She grabbed her shirt, clutching the linen fabric in her hand. "Who?"

"The police were involved. I was just talking with the lady who was at the table."

"Anna?" Monique frowned. "What happened?"

An uncomfortable warmth slammed my body as Monique and I exchanged stares for a tad second too long. It was almost like she knew I had to know more.

Monique broke her gaze, glancing down the hall. "I think I need that free drink. Someone at the conference knows something."

She started to walk away, then stopped and spun around.

I was kind of ready for her to go.

"Mrs. Patterson, it was good to see you. I will tell Daddy I saw you. He does miss his old friend." Then she added, "I'm happy for Cedric. I hope his bride makes him happy."

With that, Monique Sanders strutted off.

I thought that was big of her to say. From my recollection, Cedric's breakup with Monique was one of the more spectacular ones. Cedric's BMW suffered slashed tires. The woman rang Cedric's phone so much he had to change his number. He even spoke of her showing up at his practice and home like she was stalking him.

Leesa had described the woman as being "ratchet," a term the young folks liked to use. Drama queen to the tenth power was the way I called it.

Finally, it all stopped. Monique seemed to face the facts.

The few minutes I talked to her left my mind whirling with unease. As my thoughts gathered, it dawned on me that Monique had provided a possible explanation of why Darius was here last week. He'd come to visit and support

Monique while her father Kendall was probably hospitalized.

Okay, so maybe he wasn't stalking Carmen last week. But after Darius ran into Carmen, he'd been determined to see her again. And, there were still missing pieces. Like, how did he figure out Carmen's phone number? And how in the world did Darius know to find us at the bakery yesterday morning? And even more so, was he really following us?

Chapter 10

I glanced at my phone. It was almost four-thirty, and traffic had probably picked up considerably. I could check on Carmen. But no, I couldn't do that. I mean what would I say to her?

Carmen, I just ran into the woman that Cedric was thinking about marrying five years ago. Of course he came to his senses or else he wouldn't have found you, the love of his life.

I'm not a woman who really believes in coincidences, but I realized my unease had to do with one simple fact. Carmen's ex-husband Darius was dead and she had found him. Cedric's ex-girlfriend Monique, who went a bit psycho some years ago was looking for her boyfriend Darius. I was having a hard time trying to process this small world scenario.

What if Monique had found out this information? It'd been five years, but the woman still didn't strike me as stable.

Then it dawned on me. *Had Cedric ever told Carmen about his past?* My son was pretty upset about the bombshell Carmen dropped on him, but most of Cedric's past love interests were still here in Charleston. Did it ever occur to him that his own past may prove to be far worse?

A headache was determined to slam me to the ground.

I'd never had an ex anyone. Ralph was my one and only. That sounded crazy in the world we lived in, but I didn't know about any other men. Okay, I had these weird moments with Amos.

I mean Amos was handsome, despite being in his sixties. I'd always been a fan of Harry Belafonte, and Amos resembled my favorite actor. Being a retired detective, he had experiences I could have never dreamed of outside my years in a classroom.

Over the past two years, Amos had grown to be a lot more than a neighbor, but I wasn't ready to fully commit to something more. I was sixty-one and romance seemed to be something in a novel, not real life.

I snapped my thoughts away from Amos. I was still standing in the hallway where Monique had just left me.

Good Lord, help me! It was time to go home.

I strode down the long hallway that led away from the conference rooms. As I approached the hotel counter, I noticed the young man with the reddish bow tie still checking in guests. The lobby seating area was filled with conference attendees who appeared to be enjoying happy hour. I didn't see Monique and didn't want to run into her again.

A thought flashed in my mind that I should have ignored. I'm a person with good sense and I could slowly feel a sense of curiosity growing inside me.

What was Carmen thinking as she entered the hotel this morning? Was she scared as she headed to the elevators?

Instead of heading out the glass doors towards the parking lot, I proceeded to walk straight past the check-in counter towards the four elevators. No one else stood waiting. I'm not sure what I thought I was doing, but I pressed the up button and expectantly waited for one of the elevator doors to open. It didn't take long for the doors to slide open on the second elevator to my right.

I moved towards the elevator but stopped.

Eugeena, what are you doing?

I didn't have long to ponder my craziness before the stainless-steel doors began to close. I leapt through the doors right before they shut. Breathing hard, I smashed the number eight.

Surely, no one should be on the eighth floor. There was a crime scene. But I knew there were probably guests already assigned to rooms on the eighth floor. Rosemary said that particular suite wasn't available.

When the elevator doors slid open on the eighth floor, I really expected to see someone, like a deputy questioning my presence. But no one was in the hallway. I stepped off and turned to the left, studying the signs on the wall in front of me. Room 828 was to my right. I peered to my left to see if any guests were in the hallway, then swiveled my neck to the right as if I was about to cross a street.

Not a single person was in sight. I couldn't hear voices or even a television coming from any of the rooms.

It was too quiet.

Okay, Eugeena, turn your behind around now and leave.

My feet remained planted where I stood.

I knew the crime scene investigators and even Detective Wilkes could be on this hallway doing their jobs right now. What was I going to do if they saw me?

Despite my worries, my feet began moving closer to room 828. The suite was at the very end of the hallway. A wall jutted out into the hallway providing more privacy to the suite compared to the other rooms. As I stepped closer, a prickly feeling like fingers graced the back of my neck.

This scared me. When I was scared, I knew to reach for someone who was bigger than my fears. So, I did something I honestly hadn't thought to do all day.

Forgive me, Lord!

I whispered a prayer for Darius Randall. I'd only briefly met him face-to-face yesterday morning at the bakery. And almost twenty-four hours later, the man was killed on this very floor. I prayed for his soul to be at peace with God.

The man Carmen once loved and then feared. The same man Monique seemed to love and was desperately searching for.

I gulped and rounded the corner to view the room number. Crime scene tape was plastered across the door. How interesting that the man was killed in a room that was basically not visible from the rest of the hallway. I'm sure Darius Randall paid well for the privacy offered by the suite.

I turned back towards the door with 827 embedded on the side wall. From the angle of 827, it wasn't possible to see room 828. Still, if anyone was in 827 earlier today, they had to hear or see all the commotion in hallway. Next to the suite was 826. Did no one hear an argument or hear Darius crying out? Would the man have cried out after being struck on the back of the head? Maybe he felt a sharp pain and then only blackness.

My stomach was starting not to feel so good.

I turned to head back down the hall, praying no one would open their door. I wanted to steal away as quietly as I had come. I headed back to the elevator, thinking about Carmen. For some reason, I couldn't remember her telling us her actions after she found Darius, only that she called the police.

Did she run out the room and head straight to the elevators? Did she have the sense not to touch anything in the room? How long did she wait before she called the police?

I wasn't a detective by profession, but I watched my share of *Law & Order*, *Murder She Wrote*, *Matlock*, you name it. I knew television was not real.

My son's fiancée finding her ex-husband dead was very real.

I took a breath and pressed the elevator button. This time none of the elevators were close to the eighth floor.

As I waited, I thought about Monique. She'd been calling Darius. If they'd dated for a whole year, surely she knew his hotel room number. Monique claimed she was busy with her father's illness. *Was she with her father twenty-four hours a day?* Something else had to have gone down between Darius and Monique for the couple's communication to go sour after Monday night.

While I pondered Monique's relationship with the deceased, I noticed the second elevator on my right, the one I'd stepped off of a few minutes ago slowly ascending. I had learned a lot since arriving at the hotel almost two hours ago. I peeked at the conference program I'd swiped from downstairs and flipped a few pages in. The face of Darius Randall stared back at me.

He grinned, looking debonair. According to the ad, Darius was the opening keynote speaker on Monday night. This guy was kind of a big deal. I remember that Hudson woman saying how he was hard to book for the conference.

When the elevator slid open, I moved towards the elevator, not really looking up like I should've been. I noticed someone's feet stepping off the elevator, moving towards me, and I lifted my head. As recognition of the face hit me, I dropped the program and all the brochures in my hand. Backing up, I clutched my chest in hopes of slowing down the fast, erratic beat of my heart.

Chapter 11

My body felt electrified from the shock. "What in the world are you doing here?"

Amos walked off the elevator and reached down to pick up the pile that fell out my hand. The elevator closed behind him, and he gazed at me. "I came to make sure you weren't doing anything crazy, woman. What are you doing on this floor? There's a crime scene down the hall."

I placed a finger on my lips. "Shhh, someone might hear you." I took the papers from him. My heart was still beating super fast, but I was glad it was only Amos. A few minutes earlier, I'd been thinking about the man. I certainly wasn't expecting him to check up on me.

But then again, I should have known.

I wasn't sure if I should be pleased or worried. "Did you follow me?"

"I remembered you said you had a friend here at the hotel. I went to check on a few things with one of my contacts at the police station and decided to come by here. I also know a few people who work here."

He winked at me, making my face feel flushed. My

cheeks were warm from being scared to death. I did like it when he winked. Despite his scolding, Amos's smile lit up the hotel space.

"I've been in the lobby for a while, checking out the guests. A lot of people were talking about this morning and how there were police everywhere. Folks are creeped out about staying here. Anyway, I just so happened to see you enter the lobby. Seemed like you were trying to make a decision." He squinted his eyes. "Then I guess you decided because the next thing I knew, you were walking towards the elevators."

I felt sheepish that Amos had caught me. "Well, I wanted to experience what Carmen felt this morning."

"I have something better. Follow me." Amos pressed the elevator down button.

"Where are we going?"

He didn't answer, so I just followed him onto the elevator. Instead of pressing "L" for the lobby, he pressed the number seven.

"Why are we going to the seventh floor?"

"To check out the suite."

"You mean a suite like the one Darius was staying in?"

"That would be correct. The layout is the same."

The doors opened and we both stepped into the hallway. A couple stood waiting for an elevator. They smiled at us. I tried to smile back, but I was suddenly conscience of the fact that I was walking towards a hotel room with Amos. Something about this made me more nervous than me walking by myself towards the crime scene.

Amos walked briskly and was practically halfway down the hall. I walked faster to catch him, hoping we didn't run into anyone else in the hallway. We arrived at the end of the hallway. 728 was cornered off the exact same way as 828 above. I watched as Amos produced a key.

"How did you get the key?"

He winked at me. "I told you, I know people too."

I wasn't sure I liked him winking at me this time. The wink seemed to take on a different meaning as I stepped inside the hotel suite behind him. My daughter's recent taunting, 'Mom has a boyfriend,' sprung to mind and I almost turned around.

This is not what it seems, Eugeena. Just walk in, look around and get out.

Once we were both inside, Amos closed the door behind us. We stepped into an area that resembled a living room with a plush couch and large flat screen television. Off to the left was a kitchenette area with a sink, microwave, and coffee maker. There was a full fridge with an ice maker, and bar stools lined a counter that separated the kitchenette from the living room.

I'd noticed it had grown darker outside since I arrived, but light still shone through the opalescent curtains. A door stood open on the right. I walked towards the door and entered a bedroom with a large king bed.

Neither one of us had spoken a word since entering the suite.

I cleared my throat trying to sound business like. "So Carmen said the door was open. She pushed inside and walked in. Carmen had to see Darius in the bedroom." I walked all the way into the bedroom, expecting to see blood on the floor. I don't know why, since the real crime scene room was upstairs. I peered up at the ceiling. That man's body had been lying right above. I wondered if anyone was in this room at the time.

Did they hear a loud thump above?

I looked over at Amos who seemed to be observing each area of the room. "Do you know if anyone was in this room? They must have heard something above them."

Amos shook his head. "The couple who had this room checked out early this morning to catch a shuttle to the airport. I have someone trying to track them down. If they did hear something, especially if it was much earlier than when Carmen arrived, that could help. This case needs witnesses."

"Wow, you've been busy. Well, I have something for you too." I remembered the brochures in my hand. I placed them on the bed and pulled out the conference program. "Darius Randall was here for this conference. Look, he was the keynote speaker on Monday."

Amos took the program from me.

As he looked, I relayed what else I had learned, even about Monique Sanders. After I explained that Monique was Cedric's former girlfriend, Amos looked stunned.

"Are you serious?"

I nodded my head, "Oh yeah. He almost proposed. Thank goodness something in his gut warned him." I didn't add I was very helpful with influencing my son's decision.

Amos appeared puzzled for a moment. "You said she was looking for him? She's Darius' girlfriend?"

"It's what she said. Although, I have to say I thought she should have known where his room was located. I can see her wanting to escape being at her dad's house, you know taking care of him. Maybe sneak away with the boyfriend to his fancy hotel suite."

"I think you're on to something. So, Cedric obviously broke up with her. How did she take it?"

I shivered. "Not well at all, she slashed his tires. Cedric

ended up changing his cell phone number because she kept calling and calling. I think she bothered him for weeks afterwards. Then she just stopped, like all the steam ran out of her."

"Sounds like she was vindictive." Amos rubbed his hand across his balding head which I'd noticed was absent of his usual caps.

"Rejection is not an easy thing, but she did have her heart set on Cedric proposing. Do you think she already knew something happened to Darius, but wanted to pretend as if she didn't know anything just for show?"

"In my years as a cop, people will find ways to hide the truth. But, if she was as close to Darius as she says, I'm sure someone would have reached out to her. Keep in mind, the detective and her team are still going through Darius' phone and emails."

"So, you think there's a chance Detective Wilkes will turn away from focusing on Carmen?"

Amos gazed at me with warm eyes. "It's unfortunate Carmen came up first as a person of interest. Detective Wilkes is a good cop. She will turn over every part of Darius Randall's life."

I sighed deeply, the day's events weighed on me. "I now know Darius had to be in town earlier to see Monique's dad or at least she claimed he was here to support her. My friend said he ordered room service for breakfast every morning and liked the room cleaned daily. He'd hung around the hotel enough for the staff to notice him. I'm wondering if someone noticed if he had visitors."

Amos nodded. "Someone should be questioning the hotel staff a bit more about his activities. I can get on that." He looked back at the program. "It's also possible someone at the conference, maybe someone he knew, could have killed him. Could be a long shot, but someone living out of town would make a perfect escape."

That frightened me. The case could go unsolved. "And anyone in this hotel could have had an advantage. You said they didn't find the murder weapon, suppose someone just wrapped it up and took it with them or disposed of it right here in the hotel?"

Amos tilted his head, as if weighing what I said. "All possibilities. I'm sure Detective Wilkes has people searching the hotel. They're probably trying not to be conspicuous about it." He frowned, observing the bedroom surroundings. "I wonder what the killer hit him with though?"

I walked over to a lamp on the table behind me, but it wouldn't budge. I tried to lift the lamps on either side of the bed. "These are all bolted down. Maybe it was something they brought with them."

Then it dawned on me. I went over to the closet, and there was one object with enough force to do some real damage. I reached in and pulled out a staple element in most hotel rooms. "What about the iron?"

Amos folded his arms. "It's a possible weapon if the iron was already down from the closet. I can check on that detail."

"You mean the iron would have sat on the ironing board in plain sight for the killer to grab? Darius must have known this person well to let them in or maybe they snuck in." I shook my head. "No. They would have to have a key."

Amos said, "I believe it's a person Darius let into the room. He turned his back on them, not realizing he'd upset them in some way. Or maybe he didn't care that he upset them. Seems like he was a callous sort of guy. Angry and upset, this person chose a weapon in the room."

"It could have been a woman. The problem with all these theories is Carmen is the only one who went to see Darius the police know about. We have to find out more about Monique. From what she was saying, it sounded like she'd been looking for him to return her calls. He was upset with her about something that happened Monday night. I don't know if he was purposely ignoring her. That could have made her upset, given her motive."

I stared at the man's smiling face on the inside of the program. He looked polished and debonair. Probably wooed the audience on Monday with his speech. He didn't really look like the monster of a man Carmen described.

Maybe Darius really hadn't changed so much. Was he purposely hiding from his girlfriend or was Monique trying to hide something?

The mysteries surrounding Darius Randall seemed to grow.

Chapter 12

I took a right onto my street heading towards home. After pulling into my driveway, I examined Amos' house on the right side, but his lights were out. He hadn't returned home yet. I was grateful that Amos had stayed on top of the details and for his police contacts. As always, Amos was more than willing to offer his investigative experience. I didn't regret the afternoon snooping adventure in the hotel suite either, though I was starting to get a little curious about Amos's contacts.

They were obviously way better than mine.

I turned towards my neighbor on the left. Louise Hopkins had been my neighbor for the majority of the thirty-five years I lived in Sugar Creek. I'd watched her son grow up and unfortunately be murdered in the same house only a year ago. Before his untimely death, William Hopkins had placed his mother in a nursing home and was looking to sell the house. But Louise, who didn't have anything wrong with her despite being old, moved back into her home with a newly acquired granddaughter as her housemate. To see the two women's close relationship, it was hard to imagine they'd only been aware of each other for a year.

The lights were lit in the front of the house, and I could see the shape of one of Louise's cats on the windowsill in the picture window. Jocelyn was home too. She usually arrived home like clockwork near five thirty.

When I first met Jocelyn, she worked at Hooters, a job she tried to hide. Since moving in with her grandmother, she'd started working as a barista at a locally owned coffee shop.

Jocelyn and Carmen were close friends and maybe she didn't mean any harm encouraging Carmen to face her fears, but it sure didn't help. Like Carmen, I'd grown fond of Jocelyn too. After all, I helped the girl find out about her grandmother and late grandfather's love affair over fifty years ago. The forbidden interracial relationship took the life of Jocelyn's grandfather and left a very young Louise giving birth to a daughter she'd never known. At least not until her determined granddaughter found her.

I climbed out of my Camry and walked across the lawn over to the front door. I rang the doorbell and waited. A few seconds later, I saw Louise pull open the window curtain next to the door. When she saw me, recognition lit up her blue eyes. The front door opened, and the white-haired woman waved me inside.

"Eugeena, I told Jocelyn you would be over soon."

I arched my eyebrow. "Really? How did you guess that?"

Louise stepped back so I could enter the house. She shut the door before responding. "I have been asking Jocelyn about this man Carmen was married too. I heard she found him dead. How awful."

I followed Louise inside to the living room where Jocelyn sat with her legs curled under her. She jumped up from the couch when she saw me. "Ms. Eugeena, have you seen Carmen yet?"

"I was at her house earlier. I know you two talked already."

Jocelyn nodded. "She called me this morning and told me she found Darius. I feel awful. Last night, I told Carmen she had to face him, that she couldn't let him harass her. Now look what happened." She pointed to the television. "It's on the news."

Thinking about what Rosemary said earlier, I panicked, "Some reporters snagged the story already?" I quickly crossed over to the television to catch video footage of Darius Randall speaking at the conference. *Was this from Monday's keynote?* I spun around to face Jocelyn, "Did they mention Carmen?"

Jocelyn shook her head. "No, but it's only a matter of time. Apparently, Darius was some superstar in the world of finance. He's been on *CNN*, *The Today Show* and he even has a new book that just came out. I had no idea. I know Carmen didn't know."

I looked at the screen again seeing highlights of Darius as a guest financial analyst on various talk shows. My thoughts went to my earlier meeting with Monique. *Was she seeing this broadcast too?*

Jocelyn slumped back on the couch. "Carmen is so depressed. It's my fault for encouraging her to face him."

Louise sat beside her granddaughter and rubbed her back. "Everything will be alright, honey. No one could have known the man would end up dead."

Jocelyn shook her head. "Carmen has always been super private and sensitive. For the longest, she didn't want to admit she was adopted. She really had put Darius behind her, stuffed him away. I hate this is happening to her, especially with the wedding so close."

My chest tightened as I slowly sat on the chair near the television. "Why do you think Darius reached out to her after all these years?"

"I don't know. As far as I knew, he disappeared after the divorce and Carmen went to school."

I frowned. "Disappeared?"

Jocelyn raised an eyebrow. "To be honest, I think Carmen's dad threatened him. Technically, when Darius approached Carmen, she was still a minor. They could have pressed charges against him."

"I wondered about that. Do you remember when or how they met?"

"To tell you the truth, I don't. I had my own boyfriend issues back then. I was on and off with this guy. Carmen was kind of shy around guys, and she didn't go out much. I remember when she told me about Darius, I could tell she'd really fallen for him. Then I met him, and I couldn't believe how much older he was than her. I mean he was a good-looking guy so I could see the appeal, but I warned her to be careful."

Louise asked, "How old was he?"

"At least ten years older than Carmen, and at the time, she was seventeen. They met during our senior year." Jocelyn made a face. "I never liked him."

"Because of his age?" I asked.

Jocelyn huffed. "That and he was arrogant. Carmen refused to see it, but he was really obsessive about her. He would be there at the end of school to pick her up, which was crazy."

"What happened when Carmen's parents found out about him?"

"By the time they found out about him, Carmen was pregnant. She got her diploma and everything, but she had to break it to her parents that summer. There was no way she could start college."

"So she married Darius that summer?" I asked.

Jocelyn nodded. "Then she lost the baby. I was in school by then. She was barely married a year. She'd already been accepted to College of Charleston before she graduated. After everything blew over, she moved to Charleston and started classes the following fall semester."

"Did you know he reached out to Carmen last week?" I asked.

Jocelyn scrunched her face. "She told me she saw him at the hospital claiming to be visiting a friend. Sounded bogus to me."

I crossed my arms. "It could have been a legitimate visit to the hospital."

Jocelyn shrugged. "I didn't really know much about him. I guess it's possible he knew people around here. I mean he is a world-famous expert who traveled a lot."

I spoke up. "He was definitely here for business this week. I found that out today."

Louise and Jocelyn both stared at me.

"Yes, I've been busy. I was at the Charleston Place Hotel and there was a conference for financial advisors. From what I learned, Darius Randall was the keynote speaker on Monday." I pulled the folded program from my bag and passed it to Jocelyn. "He was here for a few days before the conference started and I know why."

Jocelyn stared wide-eyed. "You have been busy, Ms. Eugeena."

I shrugged like today's activities had been no problem. "Yeah, too busy. I met a woman today, too. Well, I already kind of knew her, but that's not important. Her dad has been sick, and she's been seeing Darius. He came here to support her."

We all sat quietly, the television now switching to national news. There was no mention of Darius Randall yet, but I knew it would only be a matter of time if the man was that famous.

Jocelyn sat with her arms wrapped around her like a frightened child. "Do you think the detectives are really looking at Carmen for murder? What about this woman Darius was seeing? Do they know about her?"

I closed my eyes feeling the fatigue from the day bearing down on my shoulders. "Being the first person at the scene of the crime, Carmen is a person of interest for sure. The detective should be digging into Darius' background, so she probably already knows Carmen's past connection. My main questions are how did Darius obtain Carmen's number and why did he want to meet with her after all this time?"

Louise offered. "The wedding? Maybe he read or heard about it somewhere and became jealous."

Or did someone else get jealous? The breakup between Monique and Cedric was pretty spectacular. She was expecting him to propose that Christmas, and he didn't. Then a few days before the new year, Cedric broke it off. For the first few months of the new year, Monique made Cedric's life hell. She showed up at the hospital, his house and even showed up at mine looking for him.

Today, I saw a somber woman seeking out a man from whom she was expecting love and support. She was on a mission to find him. Or was it all an act?

My conversation with Amos earlier reminded me that Monique could be a suspect too. If Monique already knew

Darius was dead, suppose she wanted to mingle with the other conference attendees for other reasons. What was it she said?

Someone at the conference knows something.

I could have been letting my imagination run away, but Monique knew about Cedric's upcoming marriage and she seemed way too happy for him.

Chapter 13

I woke early Thursday morning after a fitful night of trying to sleep, and I do mean early. But there was too much stirring in my spirit to fret about the four a.m. rising. The older I became, especially with the house all to myself, sometimes the Lord was the only one I could talk too. This morning, I had a lot to share with him.

This time last week I was checking off to do lists for a wedding. The week wasn't over yet, but I was already fearing it would be the worst week in a very long time. I had a growing feeling in my stomach that things were going to proceed even further downhill, so I prayed for strength and discernment. I especially prayed for anger. That one surprised me when I spilled my guts to the Lord. To be honest, I was a tad bit angry at Carmen.

Why didn't she say something before? Why did she go see that man? I was even angry with Cedric for doing what his father used to do. Run. Did he have to go off and disappear after he and Carmen argued?

I pulled my robe close over me as I watched Porgy tear around the yard. The back-porch light shone across the yard, but I couldn't tell what creature caught his eye this morning. I had no intentions of stepping out into the dark, chilly morning. I yelled, hoping not to wake my neighbors. "Porgy, get in here." The dog circled the yard at least two more times before trotting up to the door. He looked at me as though he didn't really want to come in. "Let's go. The sun isn't even up yet."

I closed the door once the dog traipsed inside. He lapped water from his bowl as I filled the coffee pot with water, my mind focused on what to do next. So much had happened in one day. The one thing that continued to bug me was why would Darius Randall reach out to Carmen after all these years? Did he have some type of conscience moment where he wanted to reach out and apologize to her? Or was he bothered by her upcoming nuptials?

After the coffee finished brewing, I poured a cup, opting to go with plain black coffee this morning. This was a small feat compared to the years of heavy cream and sugar in my coffee. I wanted to see my grandchildren grow up and be around to meet my great-grands.

I pulled out my MacBook, gifted to me earlier this year from Cedric. I quite enjoyed using the Apple computer. It reminded me of the computers I used in my classroom. I opened the Safari browser and typed in Darius Randall. I only caught a little bit of the news last night, but here on the internet I found plenty of videos about the man. He was indeed charming and articulate in person and seemed very knowledgeable about budgets, investments and finance. It was hard to imagine he was the same person as Carmen described.

I clicked around a few links finding Darius on Facebook, Twitter and Instagram. He even had his own website. Darius had recently written a book called, *Getting a Handle on Your Finances.* As I surfed through his website, I noticed he had quite a few books. He seemed to travel all the time too, based on the numerous photos displayed on his website from conferences and workshops.

In every single image, I noticed Darius wore what appeared to be an expensive suit, a closely trimmed haircut with a hint of gray at the temples and a bright white smile. He was a handsome man. There was no way he hadn't moved on since marrying Carmen. I suspected he continued to like his women much younger than him.

I decided to return to Facebook. I preferred Facebook and didn't really pay much attention to any other social media. Besides, I knew everyone posted their business on Facebook. I mean, I didn't. I did like to post and see pictures of my grandbabies.

As usual, I spent a few minutes more than I intended on the feed. Junior's twin boys were getting so tall now, inheriting their height from their grandpapa, Ralph. The boys were almost eleven and didn't visit as often, only summer vacation and the holidays. Though Leesa lived less than ten minutes away, her two children were growing way too fast. Keesha was officially in first grade and Tyric was a rambunctious two-year-old.

I tore myself from watching funny dog videos. It was so easy to get distracted.

I purposely typed in Darius Randall in the Facebook search bar. He appeared to have one of those pages you can like and a personal page. I went for the public figure page. As I scrolled through the page, I saw posts dated Monday. Darius was signing books at the conference. I recognized the interior walls of the Huntington room that Rosemary had shown me yesterday at the Charleston Place Hotel.

There were many photos of Darius posing with

attendees that appeared to be fans of the man. All of these people had no idea what kind of man he really was, entrapping and almost destroying a young woman's life. Why would he mess with his own fame to come back to haunt Carmen? This really didn't make sense to me.

The sun had started to peek through the window over the kitchen sink. It was Thursday, the day the conference ended. I glanced down at the time on the MacBook, almost seven thirty. The conference would officially be over at noon according to the program. Many of the attendees were probably gone if they had caught early morning flights.

Could Darius's killer be someone from out of town? How convenient if that were the case?

I decided to visit Darius's personal profile. I needed to know more about the man's life, not the persona he shared with the world. Was he married? Did he have children? He was close to forty now so he had to have some type of personal life. That was unless he was like my Cedric who dated sporadically, enjoying bachelorhood until his heart was snagged by a certain tall, beautiful resident.

Darius's personal wall had a different feel. There was one photo of him at a book signing. But as I scrolled, he appeared more laid-back dressed down in a shirt and jeans in most of the photos. I stopped on one photo where he appeared next to an older man.

I knew this man. The drastic change in Kendall's appearance shook me. No wonder Monique seemed so upset. Despite her father's tired, sunken face, his bright smile refused to be dimmed. He wore a bright blue robe and what could have been a wheelchair handle protruded behind him in the picture. I needed to see Ralph's old friend.

I peered at the dates on the photo and noticed the post was from last Thursday. Carmen said the first time she saw Darius, she ran into him at the hospital. I wonder if Darius was just as surprised as Carmen to run into her at the hospital?

That still didn't explain why Darius seemed to be following us on Tuesday. How did he know Carmen was at the bakery and later at the restaurant? That man was seeking out Carmen, no doubt. I recalled something desperate in his eyes.

Could he have been trying to warn Carmen about something? Or someone? I sat up straight in my chair. Maybe he told Monique about running into an old friend, more like his ex-wife. Monique's response may have been quite negative. She did claim to know about Cedric's upcoming nuptials.

Maybe Darius wanted to warn Carmen about Monique's bitterness.

Slow it down, Eugeena. I watched way too many detective shows; my mind was running all over the place with theories.

I kept scrolling until I came across what I was really looking for — photos of Darius with other women. I found one and then decided to view all the photos. There were plenty. Darius was not always with the same woman. Sometimes, he was standing between two women.

I shook my head. "He certainly didn't mind appearing to be the ladies' man on his Facebook page." Which would not have made a woman like Monique very happy. Was Monique seeking out Darius, suspicious that he might have been with another woman? If that was the case, *that woman* had plenty of motive for knocking Darius upside the head.

Most of Darius's social media photos appeared to be taken at events. Some were outside in a backyard, while others were taken inside a beautiful home. I soon came across a photo of Kendall Sanders again. He looked healthier than in the previous photo. The photo was posted last March. This time Kendall stood on one side and Darius had his arm around Monique. This was the first photo on his personal profile I found of Darius and Monique. She said they'd been dating about a year, but they must keep their relationship pretty private.

I leaned forward and stared at her face. Monique's hair was held back showing off a ruby red lipped smile, and she wore oblong shaped wire-framed glasses.

I picked up the conference program next to my MacBook and read through the schedule until I came across a familiar name on the program. Monique had introduced the speaker on Monday night. Often times, from my experience, the person who introduced the speaker knew them well. Sometimes well enough to talk without reading a boring biography.

It was time to switch gears. I typed in Monique Sanders in the Facebook search bar. It took a few minutes, but I found her. Her personal profile was not as public. Only a few photos were posted, and I wasn't about to send the woman a friend request.

I did want to know more about her life and relationship with Darius.

Suppose she was just pretending to be looking for her beloved boyfriend, yet already knew he was dead.

Chapter 14

By ten thirty, I tried checking in with both Cedric and Carmen, but neither was answering their cell phones. It occurred to me that I hadn't heard a word from Amos since our adventure yesterday at the hotel. As I thought about it, I felt my cheeks grow warm, which was silly. I felt even sillier peering out my living room window. Amos's truck wasn't in his driveway, not that I had any business keeping tabs on anyone.

Where was everyone today?

Time passed, and I grabbed some lunch. Though I didn't really want to, I had to put my investigation on hold. There was no way I could miss my duties today.

I made sure to leave the house in time, but by the time I parked my car in the church parking lot, Willie Mae had already opened the church for the afterschool program. I entered the side door of the church that led to the classrooms and both twins stopped their conversation mid-sentence.

Why did I get the feeling they were talking about me?

It was times like this I wished some other folks had

stepped forward to volunteer. I had a few who came by when they could, like Carmen, but the Brown sisters were my regular afterschool volunteers.

I slapped a smile on my face, knowing the questions were coming. So far, no nosy reporters had found out about Carmen finding the body. The news report focused on a popular financial expert who had lost his life in one of Charleston's historic hotels. That should be news enough for the twins.

As I approached, Annie Mae watched me intently with her wandering eye. The only way I could tell the two identical twins apart was Annie Mae's wandering eye, and Willie Mae had a rounder, softer face. Both women used to drive me crazy, but our friendship had grown a bit stronger. That was definitely a God thing.

"I want to thank you both for helping out yesterday."

Annie Mae nodded. "We weren't sure you were coming today."

"It was a one-time thing, ladies. I do apologize. Were the kids on their best behavior yesterday?"

"Everyone did their homework," Willie Mae said. "The only one who gave us some trouble was that Johnson boy. He's really too big for fifth grade, you know? Looks like he should be in ninth grade."

I corrected her. "He's just a year behind. We have to be patient with him. He's the one who lost his dad last year. Remember?"

Both women nodded, but I knew what they meant. Mike Johnson had tried my patience too, but I have had many "Mike Johnson's" in my lifetime. You had to keep a firm hand, but also an open heart to the hurting child hiding behind a bad attitude.

"So are you okay with your family emergency?" Annie

Mae asked. "I didn't know if you needed me today, but I decided to volunteer again."

"Yes, I think everything is okay now, but we could always use the extra hands."

Willie Mae added, "If there is anything you want us to pray about, let us know. We're all family, you know. Church family."

"Thank you. My family could use all the prayers we can get." I added, hoping this would satisfy the twins thirst for knowledge. "This wedding business has been hard work."

Willie Mae clasped her hands together as though she cracked my secret. "So that's what your emergency was about. I do remember you saying you and Carmen were going to pick out a wedding cake."

I nodded. That was actually the day before yesterday, but I wasn't going to correct Willie Mae. Besides, I did spend time yesterday making plans for the wedding reception among other things.

Annie Mae smiled too. "We received our invitation yesterday. It's about time Cedric got married. We were getting worried about him."

Worried about him. Why would they be worried about my son? That was my job.

I didn't really have any more time for the twins poking their nose into my family business. The bus would arrive soon. I'm just glad the real reason I couldn't make it yesterday hadn't come up.

We all went to work setting up the tables for snack time. Each day when the children arrived, we provided a snack before they started on their homework. I wrote in the afterschool program grant that we would provide nutritious snacks. Occasionally, we strayed with hot dogs, hamburgers and even pizza, but those times were rare.

The sisters had already started on the chicken salad sandwiches. They often irked me, but those Brown twins could throw down on any kind of salad — chicken salad, tuna salad, potato salad, egg salad — those two were the go-to salad makers for most church events.

I grabbed an apron before taking the vegetable and fruit tray out the fridge. By the time I made sure each plate had a side of baby carrots, cucumber sticks, sliced apples and grapes, I heard the squeal of the school bus stopping outside.

Two minutes later, our twelve afterschool program participants came through the door. The patter of feet and excited voices brought back memories of the school day. I removed my plastic gloves and walked out to greet the children. I spoke to everyone, asking them about their day. The younger children answered with details while the older ones grunted responses. I asked the oldest member of the afterschool program, Shanice Abrams, an eighth grader, to say grace before everyone grabbed a plate. Once everyone was enjoying their snack, I moved towards Amani Gladstone.

The nine-year-old was a miniature version of her grandmother whom I'd visited yesterday. I noticed she'd been quiet today when she was usually bursting with details about her day.

"Hey, Amani, I saw your grandmother yesterday."

The little girl wore her thick curly hair in two ponytails. She flipped one of them over her shoulder and smiled slightly. "Did you? I love to visit Grandma at the hotel. It's a really cool place."

"It sure is. We're probably going to have the wedding reception there next month."

She frowned. "What's a wedding reception?"

"It's a celebration for family and friends after a couple gets married."

"Kind of like a party?"

"That's right, and you're invited. I know Ms. Carmen would love to have you there."

Amani frowned and looked around. "Where is Ms. Carmen? She's supposed to be here."

I froze for a minute, not understanding. "Ms. Carmen does volunteer sometimes, but I'm not sure if I had her name down for today."

Amani's face fell. "Last week when she was here, she said I could interview her about her job. I want to be a doctor just like her when I grow up."

"You do?" I had to grin at this child. Last week, she wanted to be a fashion designer. That was how children were, they changed their mind every week. "Being a doctor takes up a lot of time. I can check with her to be sure we get you on her schedule. Is something else bothering you?"

Amani shook her head.

"Are you sure? You seem really sad today, and I know it has to be more than not having Ms. Carmen here."

"It's nothing. I'm just having a bad week, Ms. Eugeena. Ms. Jones gave a pop quiz today and I don't think I did very well."

"Oh honey, I know about having a bad week." I grabbed Amani's hand. "You're so smart, I bet you did better on that test than you think. Now finish your snack and we will see what you have for homework."

I felt pretty good after talking to Amani. It would have been nice to have the bad week of a nine-year-old. Life was so much simpler. The room quieted down as many of the children finished their snack and spread out into the fellowship hall or one of the classrooms to start their homework. Willie Mae and Annie Mae stayed around to clean up and keep an eye on the children who remained in the fellowship hall.

I walked back towards the classroom used for elementary Sunday School. Two students were already seated at the table. Behind me, Amani and another fellow fourth grader entered the classroom. Once everyone settled at the table with homework, I pulled my phone out of my bag to check for messages. I'd left several messages before leaving the house, and my phone indicated I had three messages waiting to be heard. I hit voicemail to listen to the first message.

"Mom, it's me, Cedric. Thanks for checking in. I'm fine. Just busy. I'll be in touch."

I noticed Cedric didn't mention anything about Carmen in his message. That concerned me.

I'd left her a message too, but neither of the next two messages were from her.

I had missed a call from Rosemary. "Hello, Eugeena. I have good news. The Whittington room is available for October twenty-second. Stop by the office to fill out the paperwork and place your deposit. I look forward to working with you all on the wedding reception."

That was good news!

The last voicemail was from Amos. He'd left a message about twenty minutes ago.

"Eugeena, it's Amos. Hey, I found out from my contacts that Detective Wilkes has search warrants ready for Cedric and Carmen's house. Also, I'm not sure if Carmen called you, but apparently, they picked her up from her office and took her to the police station. Eugeena, make sure that girl has a lawyer, okay? Talk to you later."

"Ms. Eugeena, are you okay?"

I turned towards the small voice in the classroom. It took me a few seconds to register that all four students were watching me closely. "Yes."

Amani's eyes were big. "You look like something scared you, Ms. Eugeena."

That little girl didn't know the half of it.

Did Carmen get arrested?

Chapter 15

I rushed into the police station. *Why would Detective Wilkes do this to Carmen?*

The woman was a doctor probably seeing a patient. Did they just show up at her office and take her off to the police station? And, they had the nerve to search their house. Did they really think the woman smacked Darius on the back of his head and took the murder weapon home with her?

I didn't think it was smart of Carmen to go see Darius in the first place, but the woman wasn't stupid. There was no way this would remain quiet now. I was worried about the wedding, but now Carmen's reputation, as well as my son's, was at stake.

I went up to the counter and tried to wait patiently for the officer on duty to notice me. He finally turned around, a white-haired man with a thick mustache who looked ready for his pension.

"May I see Detective Wilkes?" I asked.

"She's busy at the moment. I can let her know who's here to see her."

"Tell her Eugeena Patterson is here and... I have information for one of her cases."

The officer nodded. "I'll let her know you're waiting for her."

"Thank you." I went over to take a seat. Of course, I didn't have anything vital to the case, but I needed to know why Detective Wilkes was so focused on Carmen. I sat down and placed my purse in my lap. I took out my phone and tried to call Cedric. Where was he? He better be delivering a baby. That was the only emergency worth not being here for his own fiancée.

Carmen needed his support now. Instead, she was stuck with me.

Almost twenty minutes later, Detective Wilkes appeared. I jumped up. "Where's Carmen?"

The woman strode towards me, her face scrunched into a frown. "We're still questioning Dr. Alpine. What can I do for you, Mrs. Patterson?"

I knew Detective Wilkes was trying to be polite, but her eyes spoke I should leave the premises. I wrenched the conference program from my purse. "Did you know why Darius Randall was in town? Instead of focusing on Carmen because she found the man dead, did you look into any of these people who stayed in proximity to the man at the hotel? Or better yet, have you talked to his girlfriend, Monique Sanders?"

The detective blinked as though I'd stunned her. "Come this way, Mrs. Patterson."

I huffed and followed the woman back to an area of cubicles. She led me to one that must have been her office. The detective indicated with her hand for me to have a seat in a straight back chair near the corner of her desk. I sat, waiting to hear what she had to say. She busied herself by moving around paperwork on her desk. I saw a photo of a young boy with red hair similar to Detective Wilkes. He appeared to be around eleven or twelve. I looked away from the photo to find her staring at me. Probably not sure what to do with me.

"Mrs. Patterson, I know you want to help your ... future daughter-in-law. Right now, Dr. Alpine is the person with the motive and—"

"Did you find the murder weapon?" I interrupted.

The detective narrowed her eyes. "I'm not sharing the details of the case with you. I simply want you to understand I have to do my job."

I sputtered, "Which includes looking at the people who Darius Randall spent his time with since last week. He was in Charleston visiting with his girlfriend, Monique Sanders and her dad, Kendall Sanders."

"Stop. Did you say Kendall Sanders?"

"Yes, do you know him? He was a banker, I think the president of the bank. He and my husband were friends, golfing buddies."

Detective Wilkes nodded. "I'm familiar with him. My dad likes to play a few rounds of golf as well," She smiled faintly. "This still doesn't change the events that happened the day of Mr. Randall's death."

"But he hung out with people at that conference." I didn't want to let the detective know how much snooping I'd been doing. "He may have appeared to be a successful financial expert, but he upset someone enough to kill him."

"Yes, and Carmen Alpine feared him, and she was certainly upset seeing him again. She went to visit a man from her past that she strongly felt was in town to destroy her life and he ended up dead."

"She found him dead."

The detective leaned in close to me. "Carmen hasn't been truthful."

I gripped the bottom of the chair with my right hand as though it was going to fall out from under me. "What?"

The detective stood. She seemed much taller than her petite height. Her eyes drilled into me. "Dr. Alpine said she arrived around 9:00 a.m. to see Mr. Randall. The hotel surveillance in the lobby showed she entered the hotel around 6:29 a.m. She was inside that hotel way before she claims. Dr. Alpine had plenty of time to go see Mr. Randall and have a confrontation with him."

I opened my mouth, but not a single word came out. I was fresh out of anything to say. As I recalled from the detective's questioning Cedric earlier this week, the timeframe for Darius' murder was between midnight and seven o'clock in the morning. Which now included Carmen's presence at the hotel.

What was Carmen doing at the hotel that early?

"Mrs. Patterson, I know you want this to work out." Detective Wilkes voice softened, "I know you were happily planning your son's wedding, but you need to come to the realization that it may not happen. Dr. Alpine was distraught, and she went to that hotel with a mission."

I still didn't know what to say. My spirit was close to being crushed. Carmen had to have a really good explanation. I knew she hadn't killed that man. Without a doubt, she needed a lawyer. I struggled to speak. "Are you finished with her? Do you plan to arrest her?"

The detective shook her head. "Not right now, but she can't leave town."

I had watched too many detective shows. "So, you have

no evidence against her? No murder weapon, just a theory."

Then I thought, *where are these cameras?* Now I knew I'd been busted going to the hotel the other day. Of course, I was on a wedding planning mission. I had Rosemary to confirm that part, but I hoped none of the rest of my time at the hotel, including my time with Amos, showed up on these cameras.

Detective Wilkes crossed her arms. "I will find the truth, Mrs. Patterson. If what I find supports Carmen's involvement in Mr. Randall's murder, I will officially charge her with first degree murder. It's only a matter of time."

"Only a matter of time? You're not even going to question anyone else. I mentioned his girlfriend, Monique Sanders was looking for him. She knew he was at the hotel."

The detective frowned, "Mrs. Patterson, you can't just make a case against anyone. You need evidence. Right now, the person who was in proximity and had motive is Carmen Alpine."

"But..."

"Let me walk you back up front, Mrs. Patterson."

She'd dismissed me. I knew she probably had a heavy caseload, but she was closing in on Carmen too fast.

We walked back up to the front, and Carmen sat in the waiting area with her arms crossed, staring off. I don't think I'd ever seen her look that lost. I walked up to her. "I can take you back to the office to get your car."

She peered up at me, surprised to see me. "You don't have do that. Jocelyn will be off soon."

It occurred to me again that Cedric should be here. "Don't be silly, I'm right here."

Carmen blew out a shaky breath and stood.

We walked out, and I'm sure the weight of the world was more on her shoulders than mine. But the joyous feeling I had for this young couple was rapidly diminishing, and there didn't seem to be anything I could do about it.

Eugeena Patterson wasn't a quitter. Just like the detective, I intended to find the truth.

Chapter 16

I pulled up next to the building that was home to the Women's Health Care Center, and the first thing I noticed was Cedric's missing BMW. I parked and cut the engine. "Where's Cedric?"

Carmen looked straight ahead as though she was dreading getting out of the car. "Probably at the hospital. Jennifer Warren went into labor this afternoon."

"Does he know? Are you two even talking?"

"Barely, and yes, he knows they took me to the police station. The whole office knows. Detective Wilkes walked in and insisted on seeing me. Thankfully, my patient had just left, but I had another one in the waiting room. Detective Wilkes preferred I rode with them to the station. So, I asked Marjorie to reschedule my patient and climbed in the back of the police car like a criminal."

"You went with them? Was that really necessary?"

"I don't know. I felt like if I resisted they would put handcuffs on me. I didn't know what to do. I was shocked. Embarrassed. And scared."

My heart was beating fast. "You need a lawyer. You really shouldn't have been in there talking to them alone."

"Don't worry. I have one now. Cedric found this guy. His name is Charles Barnaby. I will meet him tomorrow." She rubbed her head. "It all happened so fast, and I realized my mistake when I didn't listen to you and Amos the other day. For some reason, I thought they would leave me alone. Next time Detective Wilkes comes around, she has to talk to my lawyer."

I hated to ask, but it was unavoidable at this point. "So, you were at the hotel earlier than you said. Why?"

Carmen looked at me for a few moments, her body shaking. "I was looking for Cedric."

I wrinkled my nose at her answer. "Why would you think he was at the hotel? He didn't know the man was there."

"Cedric wasn't answering his phone. And..."

"And what?"

Carmen responded quietly. "Cedric knew or at least I remember telling him Darius was still in town. I told Cedric that Darius was staying at the Charleston Place Hotel. When I asked him if I should go see Darius, he turned red and stormed out."

That surprised me. "Cedric didn't seem to remember you telling him the name of Darius's hotel."

Carmen threw up her hands, her voice hoarse. "Cedric was so angry with me, I'm not sure what he heard. I just know what I said and what triggered him to walk out of the house."

I sighed deeply, not liking where this conversation had gone. I didn't need the detective looking at Cedric as a suspect too. "Is that why you were so frantic on Wednesday morning to find him?"

Carmen nodded. "I drove by the hotel early. I even went into the lobby, but I didn't go upstairs. I just walked around the lobby and then walked back out. I started feeling stupid for being there. I went home, took a shower, and had coffee. I decided to go talk to Darius anyway, find out why he was here and why he wanted to see me. Tell him to leave me alone."

"I drove back to the hotel. It was almost nine o'clock on my car's dashboard. I remember that distinctly. I walked in, scared out of my mind. It wasn't like I told him I was coming. I didn't know what to expect, but I took the elevator. When I saw the door ajar, I admit I had a strong, nagging feeling that I shouldn't go in. But I walked in and called his name several times."

Her body stiffened as she stared out the car window. "Then I saw him. Dead."

Carmen faced me. "I'm not a killer. As much as he hurt me in the past, I would've never hurt him. I had moved on with my life. I'm a doctor. I deliver babies. I help bring life into this world."

Her last statement remained in the air between us.

I help bring life into this world.

Something stung my eye. I wiped my eyes not sure where the water was coming from. I already knew in my heart Carmen would never hurt anyone. Even the man who caused her to lose her own baby years ago. The woman had let good overcome her past.

I thought about what Carmen said. "You said he didn't know you were coming?"

She shook her head. "He had no idea. It was a spur of the moment decision. I have never been good at doing anything on an impulse. You know, I went out with Darius on impulse. I'd never met and dated someone on my own.

My parents, Jocelyn and my other friends tried to matchmake me with guys, but Darius was the first guy who approached me. I knew he was older, but he liked me. I didn't give it much thought back then when it came to him."

"How about with Cedric? Was he an impulse?"

A warm smile spread across her face. "I knew I liked Cedric the first time I met him, but I hadn't been dating and didn't want to push anything. He approached me long before I decided to give him a chance. I wanted to wait. Become friends. He's my best friend, Ms. Eugeena. I just hope he really understands why I didn't tell him about Darius. I don't have any excuses for not being truthful, but I never wanted to see that man or have him near me again."

I suspected my son had his own past relationships not yet revealed to Carmen. But that wasn't my place.

At the moment, I had a deep urge to go back two days and turn the clock back to when I'd been spending my day as a wedding planner before I ever set eyes on a man who was unknown to me.

We all had parts of our past that remained hidden from others. It was all about the future. "So, are we still planning to do the bridesmaid fitting on Saturday? You know that appointment is pretty critical to make sure all the dresses are ready. We're really pushing the time here."

Carmen's eyes stared at me as if I'd lost my marbles. "Ms. Eugeena, the police just escorted me in the back of a police car to question me about the murder of my ex-husband. I have made some stupid mistakes in my life, but this week I think I have officially outdone all of the stupid mistakes I could have ever made. It's quite possible there will be no wedding on October twenty-second."

Silence enveloped the car again.

This time, Carmen broke the awkward quietness by opening the car door.

I couldn't just let her leave. "Darius was seeing another woman while he lived in Atlanta."

Carmen turned around with her legs hanging out of the car. "What woman?"

Lord forgive me. I can't go telling Carmen the woman was Cedric's ex-girlfriend.

"I met her yesterday. She was looking for Darius. He was here in Charleston to support her. Her dad's been very sick and was in the hospital last week."

Carmen pulled her feet back into the car. "How do you know this?"

I forged forward. "She told me, and there are pictures on Facebook of her, Darius and this older man who's been sick. She was also at the conference Darius was attending this week."

"What conference?"

I rolled my eyes. A flash of warmth entered my body, and I knew wasn't a hot flash. Menopause was about ten years ago. I was good and mad now, and I was getting too old for all this up and down.

"Woman, you have to fight this. Talk to your lawyer. We need to find out who was in that hotel room with Darius before you arrived. We need to dig into the man's life. I tried to tell Detective Wilkes that, but she wasn't listening."

Carmen scoffed. "Of course not. She's building the case against me. Cops want murders wrapped up soon as possible. I didn't even know Darius was some kind of celebrity. Detective Wilkes really wants to pin this on me fast."

"So, you do realize you have to fight this? Your butt is

on the line here. Your career, your wedding, your life. Are you with me here, Carmen? We can find out who did this."

Carmen shuddered and then did the craziest thing. The girl laughed. I mean she held her head back and laughed to the point I wanted to laugh.

Of course, I didn't think what I said was for comic relief.

Her laughter soon turned to sniffles. "Cedric is blessed to have you as his mom. Any other mother would have kicked me to the curve, not wanting her son anywhere near me. Are you really trying to get Cedric married that bad?"

I paused for a minute before speaking. I had to think about that statement.

"No, I've watched you two together for two years. I've seen real, genuine love. I'm no matchmaker, but God put you and Cedric together. You're about as perfect as I could imagine." I let out a breath. "Marriage is going to be the hardest thing you ever do. You are going to have to fight to stay together. There must be something special about you two for all of this to happen so close to the wedding. Call me crazy," I held up my finger, "but the devil is a liar. You two are getting married."

Carmen smiled through tears. "I couldn't ask for a better mother-in-law."

"Then it's settled. We're going to have the bridesmaid fitting on Saturday. Since we just mailed seventy-five invitations on Monday, we need to keep this party moving. People are RSVPing already."

She nodded. "Unless Cedric comes with some earth-shattering news or Detective Wilkes arrests me." She looked at me, her eyes wide with fear. "Ms. Eugeena, you have to be careful. I know Cedric doesn't like when you do this kind of stuff, but you do have a knack for it. Even though you're trying to help me, I don't want you getting hurt."

"Don't worry about me. I have Amos looking after me." *Boy, did I.* I had my own friendly neighborhood stalker. Though I had to smile when I remembered seeing Amos step off the hotel elevator yesterday.

She grinned. "Thank goodness for Mr. Amos. You know the wedding we really should be planning is for you and Amos."

Before I could open my mouth, Carmen lifted her body from the car seat and shut the car door. There was a lightness to her step as she climbed into her car. The only wedding planning I had on the brain was for Cedric Patterson and Carmen Alpine.

Amos was a good man. I would be the first to admit I couldn't do my sleuthing without him.

Marriage.

Nah! That was for these young people.

Been there, done that.

Chapter 17

I didn't often eat dessert at night, but I decided after letting Porgy out for his last walk of the night to treat myself to frozen peach yogurt. At first, I didn't like the stuff. Ice cream it was not, but I finally found a brand I liked. I sat in my kitchen scooping up the last of my yogurt and pondered the past three days.

In fact, I had a notebook in front of me. I was officially on this investigation.

If anyone found my notebook, they would have seen what appeared to be a schedule. Darius Randall's week in Charleston. My guess was the man had arrived in Charleston between last Tuesday and Wednesday. Darius had been at the hotel for over a week according to Rosemary. He was in town visiting his girlfriend, Monique and her dad, Kendall, who was suffering from colon cancer. Kendall was more than likely the one in the hospital which explained Carmen's first sighting of Darius last Thursday.

I could only assume the man spent time with people during the weekend, possibly Monique and her father.

Darius delivered his keynote speech to the conference crowd on Monday evening. When I saw Monique Wednesday afternoon, she'd been calling him all day. Monique had introduced Darius on Monday night. Why had they lost communication on Tuesday? Sometime after Monday night and up until Darius's death on Wednesday, this couple had no contact. Monique appeared to be baffled on Wednesday about Darius's whereabouts, not even realizing the man had been dead since that morning.

I went back to the program schedule I'd laid next to the notebook. The evening program started at seven o'clock and Darius's speech had to be sometime before nine o'clock when the evening event ended. On the program, an after-party was listed.

Did Darius attend the conference after-party? Or would he have gone out with a smaller group? From his social media, he didn't seem like a man who shied away from social events.

What was Monique doing? I scribbled this question in my notebook. She was the kind of woman who kept tabs on a man if she was involved with him. Would she have stayed after the conference to hang around Darius? Of course, her father was terminally ill. Her focus could have been solely on her dad.

I needed to see Monique again, which I knew wasn't a good idea. The woman was Cedric's ex-girlfriend. A woman who badly wanted to marry Cedric.

Cedric needed to know.

My mind wandered back to something Rosemary said. Darius had been staying at the hotel long enough for the staff to notice him, even catch on to his habits which included room service every morning.

I wondered what time Darius had breakfast?

I thought about the layout of the suite Amos and I entered on the seventh floor. There was a kitchenette. If Darius had already received breakfast, which usually ended by 10:00 for most hotels, his tray would have been present.

Carmen said she arrived at the hotel around 6:30 a.m. then left and came back to actually see Darius around 9:00 am. I wondered if Darius was served breakfast before nine o'clock.

It was after nine in the evening, but I decided to give Carmen a call. I knew she wasn't an early to bed kind of person. I'd been retired for two years now and still found myself on the same bedtime schedule from my years of teaching. I couldn't even lay in the bed past nine o'clock in the morning.

The phone rang twice before anyone answered. "Hello, Mom."

Sometimes I wasn't sure how I felt about caller ID. It was a good thing when you didn't want to face a caller. Not so great when you're calling your son's fiancée and he answers instead. I was in investigation mode which I knew wouldn't please Cedric.

I sat up in my chair. "Cedric, well, hello stranger. I was looking for Carmen, but it sure is good to hear your voice." I practically whispered, "Is everything okay?"

"It's as well as it can be. Carmen is sleeping. I'm sure you're already aware it's been a rough day for her."

"I know. I picked her up from the police station. Would've been nice if it was you."

Cedric was quiet.

"Are you still there, son? I'm starting to worry about this whole situation. Carmen needs you. You can't call yourself wanting to marry someone when all is well. Marriage is going to have ups and downs."

"I know. We're fine, Mom. I understand why Carmen didn't tell me about this guy. I just wish..."

"Wish what?"

"I don't know. That I hadn't left the other night. Maybe Carmen wouldn't have ever gone to see that guy."

"No, no. We can't do the blame game here. Like I told Carmen, what's most important here is to find out who else had a reason to kill the man."

Cedric yelped. "What? Mom, I told you I don't want you sticking your nose where you shouldn't."

"If your mama hadn't been sticking her nose into other people's business, you wouldn't know your ex-girlfriend, Monique Sanders, was with Carmen's ex-husband."

Silence met me on the phone.

"Cedric?"

"You're kidding me, right?"

"No. I'm not. By the way, does Carmen know about Monique? I mean you almost proposed to *that* woman."

Cedric's voice was harsh. "No. I can't believe this. I thought Monique left town and moved to Atlanta."

"Well, Kendall still lives in Charleston and it sounds like her dad is dying. She's here taking care of him."

"I had no idea. Did you tell Carmen?"

"No. I know Carmen didn't tell you about Darius, but I also know you have had a lot more history with other women. In this city, I might add. Is she aware of your history?"

"It's the past, Mom."

"Mmmmm. Suppose you and Carmen are out on the town and you ran into a former girlfriend. What would you do?"

"Okay," Cedric sighed, "look you've made your point. I get it." He paused for a moment. "You don't think Monique had anything to do with this guy's death, do you?"

"I don't know, but she did slash your tires when you two broke up."

"I would definitely like to forget that time of my life. Still, other than the strange coincidence, I wouldn't make her out to be a killer."

"She was aware of your upcoming wedding. Who knows? Maybe she found out Darius was married to Carmen. Maybe she was angry about it. The detective did describe this as a crime of passion."

Cedric blew out a breath. "Monique had an ugly temper."

"I know. I remember telling you we didn't need a bridezilla on our hand."

"That's right, you talked me out of that one."

"You're the one who came to me. You asked my opinion, but I believe you already had your mind made up, Cedric. You knew Monique wasn't the one."

"Yeah, I dodged a bullet. I'm not feeling too happy about Monique being connected to this."

"Well, you know I'm not going to stop digging. Besides, I have help. Amos knows what to do. He has tons of contacts. If he hadn't called me, I wouldn't have known what was going on with Carmen."

"Do you really think that's fair?"

I frowned. "Fair? What are you talking about?"

"Mom, everyone knows how Amos feels about you. He's going to do whatever he can to make you happy. Right now, you want to find a killer which really isn't for you to be doing. You're a retired school teacher, for crying out loud!"

"Well, would you rather let Detectives Wilkes arrest Carmen the next time?"

"I would rather things go back to the way they were two days ago."

"You and me both, son. But life ain't fair, Cedric. Do me a favor? When Carmen gets up in the morning have her call me. And be sure you go with her when she sees that lawyer. What's his name?"

"Charles Barnaby. Don't worry, I personally secured his services. He came highly recommended and will be dropping by the house in the morning to see her."

"That's good to know. What time will he be coming by?"

"I think around ten o'clock. Why?"

"Don't you think Carmen needs support?"

"He's a good lawyer, Mom. I'm sure he knows what to do."

"Goodnight, son. Remember, it doesn't hurt to pray too. I will certainly be sending up my prayers tonight."

"Goodnight, Mom."

The phone rang as I trudged up the stairs with Porgy racing in front of me. I answered thinking Cedric was calling back or perhaps Carmen woke up to return my call.

I cringed as Leesa's shrill voice penetrated my ears.

"Mama, what's going on? Why am I the last to hear about Carmen and this man?"

"Have you spoken with Cedric?"

"No, Jocelyn told me. Why didn't you or Cedric tell me?"

I forgot about Jocelyn. "I'm sorry. It's been a hard two days."

"Jocelyn said Carmen was questioned by Charleston police today about her ex-husband, Darius Randall. He's some kind of famous financial expert. I didn't even know she was married before. Does this mean the wedding is off?"

My daughter, always the drama queen.

"What? No, it's not off. I talked to Carmen and Cedric. Everything is going as planned."

Leesa whined. "I don't understand why Carmen went there to see this man. Was she having an affair?"

"Oh Lord, child. She was married to that man a very long time ago. Practically a child herself. The police should be looking at someone else for this man's death."

It was time to get Leesa off the phone. My youngest child could be exhausting sometimes. I hoped she didn't talk to Cedric because she didn't need to learn about Monique. Leesa had been the first to display dislike for the woman.

"Leesa, I'll see you on Saturday as planned. Be ready for both you and Keesha to have your dresses fitted. By the way, Rosemary called about the Whittington room. So tomorrow, go ahead and put the deposit down for the reception."

"Are you sure about this, Mama? Should we keep going like none of this is happening?"

There were times when a person had to show some faith. Right now, that person was me.

"Yes, Cedric and Carmen will be getting married. The real person who killed Darius Randall will be found. Now you go to sleep and leave this with the Lord."

After I hung up, I sank down on my bed and breathed deep and heavy. I felt tired, like all this had happened over two months instead of two days.

I hit my knees. It was time to have a serious talk with Jesus tonight. I prayed for answers and new revelations into Darius Randall's life.

Chapter 18

The next morning, I awoke with one mission on my mind. I needed to ask Carmen some lingering questions. Plus, I wanted to meet this Mr. Barnaby. If he was going to be Carmen's lawyer, I needed to know his game plan.

I pulled into the driveway, happy to see Cedric was here.

Mr. Barnaby must have been the owner of the silver Mercedes. I parked my Camry next to it. I thought it was awfully nice of the man to come by the house.

Cedric didn't look very happy to see me when he opened the door. "We're kind of busy right now, Mom."

"That means I'm right on time." I moved past my son into the living room. It wasn't like he was going to close the door in my face. He knew better than that!

A large man with smooth ebony skin and a grayish short haircut sat at the dining room table. His deep brown eyes were sharp and stared back at me from behind circular gold-framed glasses.

Carmen sat in the chair next to her lawyer. She looked up, not looking like she slept at all last night. "Hey, Ms.

Eugeena," she smiled. "Mr. Barnaby, this is my future mother-in-law. Eugeena, this is my lawyer."

Mr. Barnaby raised his eyebrow at me as though I really shouldn't be there. "Mrs. Patterson, Carmen told me about your assistance with her case."

I marched up to a chair and pulled it out, making myself at home. Everyone around the table shifted their eyes towards me. Probably not sure what to do with me, but I knew what I wanted. "Do you have any coffee, Cedric?"

Knowing it was no use deterring his mama, Cedric disappeared into the kitchen.

I turned my attention to Mr. Barnaby. "I'm so glad you're here. Detective Wilkes shouldn't have hauled Carmen off to the police station like that yesterday. She didn't have any real evidence. She should be looking at all parts of the case. You know I watched that show *48 Hours*. Is that what she's trying to do? Wrap this case up in two days. She's making mistakes."

Carmen held her head in her hands. "I'm going to be ruined. I shouldn't have left with the police yesterday. My assistant has already called me several times. My patients are concerned and want to know if I will be there for them."

Mr. Barnaby placed his hands on the table. "I'm sorry, Carmen. I'm glad you called me."

I stared at Mr. Barnaby's hands. I can't say I'd ever seen a man's hands looking better than mine, but I also wasn't one of those women who treated herself to a manicure either.

Barnaby's eyes were laser focused on Carmen. "The police have nothing but circumstantial evidence. Nothing hard core like a murder weapon or DNA. Those cameras were mounted in the parking lot. What the detective failed to say is they saw you leave seven minutes after arriving. It wouldn't have been enough time for you to go up and kill Mr. Randall."

Cedric brought me a steaming cup of coffee. He'd remembered to keep it black. I nodded my thanks and took a sip. I inquired, "So you're saying whoever was in that room had to be in there more than ten minutes?"

Mr. Barnaby turned to me. "Well, I'm not saying it's not possible, but realistically, Mr. Randall had to be having a conversation with an unknown person. The conversation turned violent. It could have been quick."

The more I listened to this so-called good lawyer, the more I wondered if he really knew what he was doing. He didn't seem to be offering anything to make Carmen feel better.

Carmen shook her head. "I'd never guess Darius Randall would turn out to be some celebrity. I looked online today, he has like 20,000 followers on Instagram. The man never read a book that I knew of and come to find out, he's authored seven books in the past eight years. He's like a saint to some people because he's helped them get out of debt and learn to live like a millionaire."

I eyed Carmen. "Well, he wasn't a saint. Someone didn't like him a whole lot since they smacked him upside the head and left the man dead." Then I remembered the real reason I came to see Carmen. "Are you sure you didn't see any evidence of another person being in Darius's room on Wednesday morning?"

She shook her head. "I wasn't really paying attention. I was pretty focused on talking to him. It had been a long time since I talked to him face-to-face."

"This may seem like a really strange question, but when you walked in, what did you notice about the room?"

Carmen bristled with nervous energy. "What do you mean?"

Mr. Barnaby stared at me as well, his eyes disapproving. *I was stepping on his turf with my questioning.*

Cedric spoke up. "Mr. Barnaby's time is pretty valuable here, Mom. Can this wait?"

I was no cop, but I knew I didn't want to lead Carmen into an answer. "No, Mr. Barnaby is supposed to defend Carmen. That means he needs to know what kind of evidence the police are building for the prosecutor. Right?"

Mr. Barnaby's gray eyebrow shot up again, but his mouth curved into a smile. "You're quite knowledgeable about the law, Mrs. Patterson."

I shook my head. "I wouldn't claim that. What I do know is details are important." I eyed Carmen. "What do you remember seeing in the room? Suppose someone else was there before you? Could Darius have had breakfast with someone? Maybe there were two plates or two coffee cups?"

She frowned. "I don't remember anything like that. Besides, if there was, then Detective Wilkes would have DNA to work with from someone else."

We remained quiet for a moment. Then Carmen said, "I do remember a tray by the door."

That's something. "A tray?"

"You know, the tray you get with room service. There was a tray by the door, but I only remember one glass."

I responded to this revelation. "So he received his standard breakfast order from room service."

Cedric stared at me. "How do you know this, Mom?"

Carmen looked baffled. "He had breakfast. What does that matter?"

I slapped the table. "It nails down the timing. You arrived at nine o'clock. He had to be dead for a while. Didn't Detective Wilkes mention a time frame starting after midnight and lasting until seven o'clock? I bet his breakfast was delivered before seven o'clock. Someone entered his room after he received and finished his regular breakfast order."

I gazed around the table. Everyone was staring at me like I'd grown a horn.

I tried to explain. "When I talked to my friend, the hotel manager, she said Darius had been at the hotel over a week. The staff noticed him because he ordered room service every morning. I bet some of the same people served him and took care of his room every day he'd been there. He seemed to be a man of routine. Darius had no qualms with letting whoever killed him into his room. Something he said made them angry. This angry person picked up an object and struck Darius on the back of the head."

Carmen rubbed her arms as if she felt a chill. "This all sounds like a great theory, but Detective Wilkes thinks they have their person. Me."

I exclaimed. "But you arrived after all of this happened." I looked at Mr. Barnaby. "Tell her. Don't lose faith. Not yet."

Mr. Barnaby nodded. "I have to admit Mrs. Patterson is thinking in the right direction. It's up to the prosecutor to prove your guilt. We can certainly present doubt about their findings... that someone else was in that room before you arrived."

I still wasn't sure I liked Mr. Barnaby. I suppose he was still thinking through a strategy, but time was of essence. If Detective Wilkes was not going to look at every option, she would settle on charging Carmen. We couldn't let that happen.

I didn't know if Cedric talked to Carmen yet, but I felt the need to point out the presence of Monique Sanders. "You know what, Mr. Barnaby, it was really great to meet you. I do need to run some errands today. Cedric, can you walk me out?"

Cedric followed me out. "You don't like him, do you?" He asked, once we were close to the front door.

I held my hand to my chest, projecting an innocence at Cedric's question. "Don't like who?"

Cedric's exasperated look told me he knew the game I was playing.

"He doesn't seem to be helping. What's his strategy?"

"He's the best, Mom. Mr. Barnaby knows what he's doing. I just wish we had hired him earlier. Carmen could have called him and maybe avoided the whole process yesterday. It's really unfair how this detective has focused on her."

"Especially when there is another woman more current in Mr. Randall's life." I peered at Cedric. "Did you tell Carmen about Monique?"

His eyebrows shot up. He glanced over his shoulder as if he was expecting Carmen to appear behind him. "Not yet. Do you think it's necessary?"

I frowned at my son. "Look who's keeping secrets now. That lawyer certainly needs to know. Of course, you need to tell her. Monique claimed the man was her boyfriend, but she didn't seem to know his whereabouts. I'm sorry, but I'm not convinced she didn't go over to there and kill him herself. She was pretty volatile when you broke up with her. What do you think?"

Cedric closed his eyes. "She had a temper, but murder.

Do you really think she would kill someone and then walk around later like she knew nothing about it?"

I shrugged. "You knew her better than me. I just remember the aftermath. That woman shook you up a bit with her behavior after the breakup. I don't think anyone's ever reacted the same way."

Cedric looked over his shoulder again. "Okay, I'll talk to Barnaby and tell Carmen." He squinted his eyes at me. "You've been really busy, Mama. You're not planning on sticking your nose anywhere else, are you? You know how I feel about you doing this. Barnaby has his own investigators."

I was sure the slick lawyer did, but I can't really say I trusted the man. For all I knew, Barnaby could have been relishing the idea of Carmen getting arrested and going to trial. He was a defense attorney.

"Don't worry about me. You stay focused on how to help support your fiancée. Tell her I will see her tomorrow at the bridal shop at ten o'clock."

My son's face appeared more nervous.

"This wedding is still happening. Understood? I know you two love each other."

I reached up to hug him. He was a grown man, but still the sensitive boy I raised. The one who grew quiet and pensive when life dealt him a blow. The boy who craved and didn't always receive his father's attention, the very man whose steps he followed into medicine. My son, for whatever reason, balked at love and commitment until Carmen Alpine caught his eye during her residency under him.

There was something special about their union. I knew it.

It was time for me to get reacquainted with someone

who had been close to Cedric. Someone, I thanked God, my son had sense enough to walk away from years ago.

Chapter 19

I'm sure the last person Monique expected when she opened her front door was me. It took me some time, but I remembered the affluent neighborhood where Monique grew up. It had been almost six years ago since I'd been here. Ralph was still alive then, and Monique had invited us over for dinner with her father.

Despite Ralph's friendship with Kendall, I knew Monique's dinner invitation was trouble for Cedric. Whether it was Monique's influence or her father's desires, they both seemed to put the pressure on Cedric that evening. That dinner was what led me to believe Monique was simply not marriage material for Cedric.

I almost had misgivings about my mission today at the Sanders' home. I could see Monique's red-rimmed eyes through the lenses of her eyeglasses.

"Mrs. Patterson, what are you doing here?"

"I was hoping we could talk."

Monique frowned. "This isn't a good time."

Before the woman could shut the door in my face, I

stretched my arm towards it. "I have some questions about Darius Randall. I believe you knew him."

Monique opened the door wider, her sad eyes flashed. "Why would you be asking about him? I've had enough of people bothering me about Darius."

"Don't you want to know who did this?"

She looked at me, narrowing her eyes. "The detective was just here. She said she had a suspect."

For a few moments, I wondered if I had made a mistake.

Carmen was supposed to be a person of interest, not a suspect. Did something change?

"Who's at the door, Monie?" A voice asked from behind Monique.

I took a breath and looked at Monique. I knew the voice belonged to her father. It had been a long time since I'd seen Kendall.

She opened the door wider and stepped back.

I wasn't sure if I should enter the house or not, but my gaze fell on the man in a wheelchair. He appeared even more frail than the picture I'd seen on Darius's Facebook page.

"Kendall," I tentatively placed a foot inside the door. "I don't know if you remember me, but I'm—"

"Ralph Patterson's wife. I remember you, Eugeena. I also remember your son, Cedric. He and my Monie were together for some time. Thought that boy would marry her."

My other foot remained outside the door just in case I needed to leave. Maybe Cedric was right. I could make sure Barnaby and his investigators did the questioning.

The man waved me inside. "Come on in. We could use the company. It's been a sad state of affairs around here."

The Sanders' foyer was immaculate, and the first thing

I noticed was the elegant staircase. It was kind of unexpected, but breathtaking. I looked around the immense home. The Sanders family was very well-off financially, always had been. Kendall's years at the bank had served him well. I remembered Ralph commenting years ago that Monique spent most of her years in private schools.

I followed Monique into the living room which appeared to be straight out of a *Southern Living* magazine. The couches were white and gray with colorful pillows placed carefully in various areas. I wasn't sure if I should sit down until I saw Monique hold out her hand towards the smaller couch. I slowly sat on the edge.

I smiled. "I really appreciate you seeing me out of the blue. I'm sorry for your loss, especially... It being so sudden."

She nodded but remained quiet. Monique wouldn't look at me, but I felt anger emanating from her body. I wasn't sure if it was grief or the fact that she really didn't want me in her father's house.

Kendall rolled up next to the couch. He glanced at his daughter then smiled at me.

Though his face was more gaunt, he was still a handsome man.

"I wish Ralph was around still. I miss him and our golf battles. You may or may not know, but I have stage four colon cancer. It's been a rough few weeks," Kendall said.

"Oh no, I'm so sorry to hear that." I glanced at Monique, who stared at the fireplace on the opposite side of the room. No fire was lit, though several photos lined the mantle above it. "I recently found out you'd been in the hospital."

Kendall nodded. "I'm hanging in there. Monique has

been a big help. I hate to see her hurting now, especially over Darius."

Monique spoke, her eyes glazed. "We were going to get married." She moved her head towards me. "This spring. I knew he would propose soon."

My heart went out to the woman. I mean really, she had her sights set on yet another man proposing to her. Maybe they'd discussed marriage and Darius told her spring would be the best time. Or maybe the woman was a bit delusional.

Either way, I felt guilty for sitting on the couch with questions lodged in my throat. But when I searched her eyes, I saw a grieving woman with a bitter face, as if someone had played a cruel joke on her.

Monique continued. "The last time we talked was Monday night. We had a fight. I had no idea Monday would be the last night I'd ever see him."

My mind was whirling. "How long had you known him?"

Kendall surprised me by answering for his daughter. "They met through me. Darius was my intern years ago. I invited him to the house for Thanksgiving during the semester he interned. He didn't have family to go home to. I wasn't sure why, but he was one of my best interns."

Kendall shifted in his wheelchair. "We've kept in touch over the years. He helped Monique get a job and settle in Atlanta a few years ago." He cleared his throat and glanced at his daughter; his eyes were troubled. "I hadn't realized you two had grown that close."

There was a hint of something in Kendall's voice. I looked from him to Monique. His daughter would not look him in the eye, but Kendall stared at her.

Her father continued. "He'd been married three times, Monique."

Anger spread across Monique's face. "What are you trying to say?"

I was stunned, and for a minute I felt frozen. *Three? The man was married three times!*

Kendall paused for a moment before replying. "Darius was disturbed. He was good at what he did in the finance world, but he had his own demons. I hate that he lost his life, but I'm not sad that you're not walking down the aisle with him."

Monique jumped up from the couch. "You are cruel. You're sick, and I don't mean because of that chair. I can't believe you would say that to me." The woman stormed out of the room.

It took me a second to realize my mouth was open. I closed it and tried to refocus on the reason for my visit. Of course, with Monique gone, I couldn't talk to her anymore.

I narrowed my eyes at Kendall. "I'm assuming you knew about his past marriage to Carmen Alpine, my son's fiancée?"

Kendall's eyes focused on the glass coffee table as if looking at it for the first time. "Now you've confirmed why you're here, Eugeena. If you're asking me if I knew about Carmen, yes, I knew she was his second wife. From what I remember, she was married to Darius the shortest amount of time. She got pregnant or something. Lost the baby."

"Yes."

Kendall frowned. "This woman is a suspect now."

I'm not sure how he knew this. "A person of interest. She found him."

Kendall's eyes pierced me. "What were you hoping to learn by coming here?"

"I wanted to know who else Darius was involved with? Monique said the last time she saw him was Monday. What happened? Why was he still in town after the keynote? Most speakers leave."

Kendall sighed. "He came to see me on Tuesday. As far as I knew, he was planning to leave Wednesday. He mentioned he would fly back to Atlanta on Wednesday evening."

I didn't think about Darius's plans to leave. I was curious about the timing of his visit. "What time did he come to see you on Tuesday?"

Kendall observed me before responding. "Why are you asking?"

"Because the first time I laid eyes on the man was Tuesday morning. He showed up at the bakery where Carmen and I were sampling wedding cake. Neither one of us can figure out how he even knew where to find her. Or where he got her number. Later, I want to say he followed us to the restaurant where we ate. Kendall, the man was following Carmen."

He frowned. "Well, he arrived at the hospital in the afternoon. He was upset about something, but I assumed it was because him and Monique had argued."

"Argued?"

"Apparently they argued about something Monday night. She was barely talking to me when she arrived to see me Tuesday morning. When Darius showed up at the door that afternoon, Monique left. Neither one said a word. It was like ice in my room. But you said you saw him."

So Monique did see Darius on Tuesday at the hospital. "Yes, well first you should know he ran into Carmen at the hospital, I guess when he was visiting you Thursday. I don't know why, but it seemed like he was going out of his way to try to see Carmen before he left town on Wednesday."

Kendall bit his lip. "Well, like I said, Darius had been married three times. He was an efficient worker, but troubled. I kept in touch with him. From time to time, he reached out to me. I didn't know about his marriage to Carmen until later. Really, not until after it was over; it was so brief. The man wasn't built for marriage, but he tried."

"Three times that you know of?"

"He married right out of college. I recall seeing a photo of him standing next to a blonde-haired woman. Can't remember her name, but she was a beauty. If I'm not mistaken, she was from Charleston."

"Any ideas about the third wife?"

Sanders nodded. "I met her briefly about six years ago. I think she passed away from some kind of disease... could have been leukemia. When Monique was looking to move from Charleston, I reached out to Darius and that's when he told me about his third wife."

"Looks like he was trying to find love." I added, "Even with your daughter."

Kendall's face grew grim. "I wouldn't have allowed it. Darius had some issues I wouldn't want my daughter to experience. His lifestyle wasn't what Monique needed. I just didn't realize they had grown that close. Naive of me not to see it coming, but Monique didn't need the kind of instability Darius brought with him."

Instability indeed. "Carmen lost her baby. I hate to say Darius was the cause, but he did push her down."

Kendall appeared shocked. "I had no idea. I knew the girl's parents were ready to go after him. In fact, I believe the father did. She was very young, wasn't she?"

"Yes, she was seventeen and still in high school when Darius approached her. Eighteen when they married." I paused. "Did Darius have children with either of the other two wives?"

"I don't think so."

I thought I heard something behind me. *Was Monique returning to the living room or was she listening to the conversation?*

It was time for me to go. I stood. "Thanks for seeing me, Kendall. I'm sorry you and your daughter lost Darius. Sounds like he made a great contribution to the world, despite his personal issues."

"I knew he was ambitious, but I would have never imagined him as some financial rockstar." He wheeled towards the front door and I followed. I peeked back towards the staircase almost expecting to see Monique sitting on the stairs. I wondered if she had been there. If so, she knew all about Darius and his past with Carmen now.

I really wanted to speak to Monique more, but I was doubtful we would talk again. The young woman appeared to have shut out her own father after his words. I'd witnessed her bitterness over the breakup with Cedric. Here she was close to marrying someone she loved. Someone she apparently had known for many years since Darius interned for her father.

It would have been nice to know more of the history Monique had with Darius.

I grasped Kendall's hands before walking out the door. "I will keep you in my prayers, my friend. You were a good friend to Ralph."

"I appreciate your prayers, Eugeena. I hope everything works out."

Another thought occurred to me. "Kendall, how did

you find out about Carmen being questioned by the police?"

"Well I have a friend on the force. One thing about playing golf, the circle of friends can expand to all kinds of fields."

That's right, Detective Wilkes did mention her father knew Kendall. It occurred to me that the detective did follow-up from my office visit yesterday.

"So you told the detective about Darius visiting you on Tuesday?"

He nodded. "I did. It was the last time I saw him, unfortunately."

"He didn't mention his plans for the evening?"

Kendall eyed me. "No, he didn't. But I know his plans didn't include Monique if that's what you're really here for, Eugeena. They were still upset with each other. Monique was beside herself. She'd called and left messages Tuesday evening. I knew she wanted to go find him, but I was discharged from the hospital Wednesday morning. She stayed here to get me settled back at home."

I smiled, realizing Kendall had provided me with his daughter's alibi. *Did he feel my suspicions about his daughter?*

I said goodbye again. It occurred to me as I headed to the car that I was moving back to square one. I had no ideas about Darius's life or who else he would've let into his room. But, I was more aware about his past.

Carmen wasn't his only wife. In fact, she was wife number two. There had been two other wives, one deceased. Did Monique not know this? Did she know she was desperately trying to become wife number four?

After I climbed in my car, I looked up at the Sanders' house. A curtain in one of the windows moved. *Was that Monique?*

Suddenly feeling like I had just dropped myself into a *Lifetime* movie, I picked up my phone and dialed Amos's number. He answered on the second ring.

"Eugeena, where are you?"

"I just left an old friend's house. Someone who knew Darius. You know those contacts of yours?"

"Yes."

"Marriage licenses are public, right?"

Amos cleared his throat. "Why, you need to look up one?"

"Or three. Our victim was married three times. One of those, of course, was Carmen which we know."

Amos let out a whistle on the other end. "This man was something else, wasn't he?"

"Oh yeah, sounds like he was working on wife number four. Now somewhere in there, I'm thinking a woman has to be involved in Darius's death, just not Carmen."

"I'm on it. Are you sure you're safely out of trouble, Eugeena?"

I peered up at the window again. The curtain seemed to be closed. What I saw a few minutes before could have been my imagination.

"Don't worry about me. I'm heading home right now. See you soon."

I ended the call and started the engine. As I drove away, I prayed for Kendall's health and his daughter. In the back of my mind, something felt off about Monique Sanders.

I didn't think she was mentally fit. Which meant she could be really dangerous.

Chapter 20

Despite the past week, we all beamed with tears cradling our eyes on Saturday morning as Carmen stepped up on the platform in the middle of the bridal shop. Surrounded by me, her mother, Leesa and Jocelyn, Carmen spun around in her floor length fitted dress. Every curve well defined, the material glittered under the shop's bright light.

While her face appeared strained, Carmen's smile broke through as she repositioned the veil around her bare shoulders.

Carmen's mother, Frances Alpine, had tears streaming down her round, peachy face. The more I saw Carmen and Frances together, the more I noticed how hard it was to tell that Carmen was adopted. She really looked like Frances's biological daughter.

Frances patted her hands together and exclaimed, "Carmen, you're beautiful. Just beautiful."

The mother and daughter connected with their eyes across the room.

This had been worth the effort for all of us to meet this morning.

I felt a tug on my pants and peered down at my granddaughter who was grinning. Keesha wore her flower girl dress along with shiny black patent shoes. "Carmen is pretty," she said.

I bent down. "She sure is and you look pretty in pink too."

Keesha scrunched her face. "My shoes don't feel so good though."

I peered down at the shoes, not sure why Leesa insisted on the stiff shoes. They were the same shoes Leesa despised when I made her wear them to church as a little girl. "We will talk your mama into getting you another pair of black shoes."

I stood and looked over at Leesa and Jocelyn, both wore the same shade of pink as Keesha. The younger women's dresses were not for a little girl. They were similar to Carmen's dress, showing off their curvy figures. Not a bad selection for bridesmaid dresses. I'd seen worse in my sixty-one years. The wedding planning had come together well.

With the exception of the lingering murder that sat like an elephant in the room, that is. The girls headed to the dressing rooms to change, and I looked at Frances. I really didn't want to ask, but Frances knew more about Carmen's first marriage than most.

"Frances, you mind if I ask you some questions while Carmen is out of earshot?"

She turned to me, her eyes filled with questions. "You want to ask about the first marriage, don't you?"

I shrugged. "I'm sorry. I'm sure Carmen marrying my

son has been a completely different experience. And with recent events..."

Frances shuddered. "I can't believe that man. How did he think he could walk back into her life again?"

"I heard he'd been married before Carmen. Did she know that before she married him?"

Frances shook her head. "No." She turned around to make sure the girls were still in the dressing room. "You know Carmen was pregnant. Carmen thought it was the right thing to do, but she had her own reasons. You know so many young girls get pregnant and the dad is never in the picture. Darius was so much older. It was like he took over Carmen's life. She had barely graduated high school, and now she was going to be a mother. He was, or appeared to be, a wealthy man, so we knew the baby would be taken care of. That was until Carmen called us one night. She'd fallen. First, she said he pushed her. She kept changing her story. Anyway, after that night, we wanted her to leave him."

Frances caught her breath. "We hired an investigator. We should have done that in the beginning. He told us about Darius's first marriage. When they divorced, the first wife claimed Darius had hit her."

My eyes shot up. "So he had a history of domestic violence?"

Frances's eyes fluttered as if to hold back tears. "Yes, we should have looked into his background sooner, but it all happened so fast. Carmen was shy. You know we adopted her when she eight. Quiet girl who like to read, even back then. She was a tall, pretty girl. People expected her to play basketball, but she was no athlete. Academic though. She didn't blossom like other girls. Darius caught her while she was vulnerable."

I shook my head. "What happened to this first wife? Did you find anything? Her name perhaps?"

Frances sighed. "I don't recall offhand, but I can find the paperwork. I'm sure Steven kept it. We never told Carmen. She finally started to see the real Darius on her own, thank God. She realized she'd made a mistake and came to us for help. We moved her back home and then to school. Got her a lawyer to help with the divorce."

A smile crossed Frances' face. "She loves Cedric and she adores you, Eugeena. Your entire family. You have no idea how much it means to have her married into a loving family like the Pattersons."

I wasn't prone to public emotions, but Frances almost had me wanting to do an ugly cry. Thank goodness Keesha opened the dressing room door and ran towards me. "Look, Grandma, I have another pair of shoes."

I looked into the shoe box Keesha had opened. A nice soft pair of black leather shoes peeked out from the tissue paper.

My daughter approached and gave me a side eye. "I couldn't stand those hard shoes when I was a little girl."

I laughed and reached for my daughter, and then my granddaughter, grabbing them in a bear hug. The Pattersons were by no means a perfect family, but I loved my children and grandbabies.

I peered over as Carmen reached down to embrace Frances. The warmth in the bridal shop felt good, just like it was supposed to feel.

In the crevices of my mind, I knew the feel good moment wouldn't last. I prayed for strength because I had no way of knowing what was coming next.

I just knew it was coming.

Chapter 21

Sunday morning service was the first time in a while that most of my children had attended. I often never saw Cedric at a service, but today Carmen sat next to him on the end of the pew. Carmen mentioned her mother had driven back home last night. The young woman seemed to appear more relaxed having her mother around yesterday.

Leesa sat in the middle with Keesha on one side and Tyric on the other. Keesha colored quietly during the sermon while Tyric wiggled for most of the service, until he fell asleep with his head against my arm.

Amos sat next to me, which was feeling more comfortable than I would admit. When we first started sitting together at church I remained distracted due to the stares and grins. I mean we were sitting next to each other in God's house. We were really good friends. At least that's what I told the pastor and any other nosy church members.

Amos was practically in some ways a part of the family. My children and grandbabies had adopted him.

Now, he didn't replace Ralph at all. But his presence filled an empty space.

After service, we walked down the hall waiting to greet the pastor, and Annie Mae and Willie Mae showed up at my elbow. The twins always managed to find me either before church or after. Today wasn't my day to be an usher along with them so they had to make an effort to approach me.

Willie Mae whispered loudly. "I'm surprised your family came today."

I whirled around and looked at both sisters. "Why in the world would I not come to church today?"

Annie Mae interrupted. "Well, not you, but her."

I turned. "Carmen?"

Willie Mae nodded. "We heard the police took her away in the police car on Thursday."

Annie Mae leaned around me as if to observe Carmen more closely. "What's going on with your family, Eugeena? Why did the police pick up that girl?"

I sucked in a breath, making sure I remembered I was standing in the Lord's house. "It was a misunderstanding. No need to worry. She's a grown woman getting ready to marry my son. Not a girl."

With that, I turned and caught up to the line. Amos was shaking Pastor George Jones' hand. I reached out and grabbed the pastor's hand.

Pastor Jones held my hand and peered into my eyes. "Everything okay? If you need your church family to pray, let us know."

I smiled, feeling my stomach tense. Something was going on. "Our family can always use prayer. Thank you, Pastor."

He nodded. "The Lord will provide a ram in the bush. Keep the faith."

I walked away trying to recall what kind of ram. Would it be the ram that would keep the focus of last Wednesday's murder off Carmen?

I moved towards Amos. "Something's going on. People seem to know about Carmen being questioned by the police on Thursday."

He nodded. "It's possible. People talk. There could have been someone in the office on Thursday that spread the word."

Just as Amos said those words, I looked over to find someone staring at Carmen. Iris Canton. A nurse who had worked with Cedric since he started at the private practice owned by Ralph Patterson for years. She'd been at the practice, crying harder than me when Ralph passed away a few years ago.

I knew without a doubt she'd been talking.

I walked towards her.

My walk must have looked like I meant business, because Iris's eyes widened as though she thought I was coming to hit her. Of course, I would do no such thing outside the church. I would never hit anyone anywhere.

I still wanted to give her a piece of my mind.

She saved me from having to beg God for forgiveness later by scrambling towards the parking lot.

"Mama, everything okay?" I turned to see Cedric, Carmen and Leesa watching me. I glanced back at Amos, who appeared ready to go after me if I did something stupid. I smiled. "Let's go eat."

Thirty minutes later, Cedric signed up for a table on the long waitlist at Sweet Mama's Kitchen. This establishment was barely two years old but had made quite the impression on those seeking soul food with healthy alternatives. No fried chicken here. Only baked, with delicious spices to make you forget the greasiness of a past favorite. Thirty-five minutes later, our hungry, borderline moody group of seven was seated with two tables pushed together near the back of the restaurant. By the time we all hit the packed buffet at least once, any grumpiness had begun to dissipate among forks flying and fresh yeast rolls being delivered and promptly devoured.

I was finishing up the last of my baked chicken when something like a sharp breeze floated over me. We were not sitting near a door so I wasn't sure why I was feeling this cold air. I looked up and to my shock, a person was walking towards the table. It certainly wasn't our waiter who'd been a middle-age woman definitely tipping her hair in the jet-black dye box. She was friendly enough, and I wanted to make sure she was tipped nicely.

The woman who approached stopped right in front of Cedric and Carmen. Cedric looked up. In his shock, he dropped his knife and his fork fell to his lap as he seemed to lose the use of his arms. Carmen reached out to touch Cedric's arm.

All eyes at our table, and probably a few others nearby, were focused on the woman standing in front of us. Her long hair fell over her shoulders in a mess, like the wind had whipped and personally styled it for the woman. Monique Sanders appeared ready for a fight. I scanned the restaurant for her father. Being wheelchair bound, I couldn't imagine he'd be out in public. I wished he was here. He would have been the voice of reason Monique needed as she stood with her balled-up fists across from my son.

This I could not have seen coming, but I shouldn't have

been surprised. The last five days had been one crazy thing after the other, but I was kind of hoping for a break on the Sabbath.

Monique choked out. "Cedric, you managed to ruin my life again. This time because of her." She pointed to Carmen. "Was she the reason we broke up?"

Cedric sputtered. "What? No... We didn't even know each other. What are you doing here?"

"She killed him. I know she did. The police have proof. I'm going to make sure she and you both pay."

I noticed our waiter and a restaurant manager hovering behind Monique, and I also noticed someone else.

The woman I'd met at the conference. *What was her name again?*

Anna.

She quietly came up behind Monique, looking apologetic. "Monique, you can't do this." Anna apologized, "I'm really sorry. She's having a hard time."

Anna placed her hands on Monique's shoulders, but Monique shook them off. Tears flowed down her face. She pointed at Carmen. "You did this, you killed him."

Monique bolted across the table towards Carmen. Cedric pushed Carmen out of the way and held his arms up to hold Monique back.

In a flash, Amos leaped from his seat and reached for Monique's arms which were flailing, making contact with Cedric's face. A deep red mark started to appear on his cheek.

I jumped up and pushed Keesha towards her mother. Thankfully, I heard the manager yell, "Call the police."

Monique raved like a lunatic, struggling to break free. Amos guided her down with her arms behind her. Retired or not, he was in full police mode now. I stepped back staring down at the crazed woman then peered over at my family. Leesa was holding tight to Keesha and Tyric, both kids looked frightened. Carmen held a napkin to Cedric's cheek, her face mixed with questions.

The police arrived, applied handcuffs and escorted Monique out of the restaurant.

Anna stood by clasping her hands.

"Were you two in here already?" I asked her.

She nodded and pointed to a booth that was near the door to the kitchen. "We were eating over there. She saw your family walk in and started talking erratic. Next thing I knew, she flew out of her seat. I'm so sorry. I should have tried to ask her to leave. I had no idea she would do that. I've never seen her like that before." Anna's green eyes were large and wide.

I rubbed the woman's arm. "You didn't know. Do you have her father's number? Someone should tell him."

Anna nodded. "I will call him and also see if she needs a lawyer. I'm sorry."

We were still getting stares, but most people who were around us had left or were in the process of leaving. I felt bad about the commotion during the restaurant's busiest time.

I sat down. "We should head home."

Carmen moved away from where she was tending Cedric's ugly scratch. "Who was she? This crazy woman comes out of nowhere accusing me in public of being a killer. I don't understand. I'm not a suspect."

"Monique Sanders," I answered. "She may have found out when Detective Wilkes questioned her and her father. She was Darius' girlfriend." I looked over at Cedric who looked like he might pass out. "Cedric, you did tell Carmen about Monique, right?"

The look he gave me reminded me of when he was a boy and he knew he was in deep trouble.

Carmen stared back and forth. "What were you supposed to tell me about her? Did you know her?"

I smacked my hand against my head.

What in the world was Cedric thinking?

Leesa exclaimed in her pure drama queen, spoiled younger sister fashion, "You didn't tell her, Ceddie? Good Lord, you almost married *that* crazy woman. Thank God, you didn't. I thought she was horrible before when she slashed the tires on your BMW, but this is another whole crazy. I hope she gets some help because she needs it."

Carmen stared wordlessly at Cedric, whose caramel skin seemed to glow with reddish undertones.

Well, the secret was out.

My son would have to deal with why he chose to not tell Carmen sooner. That's what he gets. You never get too old not to listen to your mama.

I wanted to know where Monique got off calling Carmen a killer in public. The woman had a temper and maybe it made her go off seeing Cedric and Carmen together out in public. Still, something about the whole scenario didn't sit right with me.

This has always been at the back of my mind, but I knew without a doubt someone was setting Carmen up to take the fall for Darius's murder.

Not on my watch.

Chapter 22

After arriving home from the Sunday dinner catastrophe, I started to put a plan in place. I'd been skirting around the issues of trying to find out more about Darius's time here in Charleston, and I was tired of not getting anywhere, especially with Monique Sanders on some blind rampage. I could only think that her father's sources were feeding him information we were not privy to.

Before heading to bed, I went to my desk and rifled through the items I picked up from the Charleston Place Hotel last Wednesday. The card I needed had been inserted inside the conference program.

Anna Hudson. Financial Advisor. Chambers Financial Group.

Monique was at the restaurant eating with Anna. The women were obviously friends. I didn't know how deep their friendship went, but Anna's apologetic actions around Monique's behavior stuck with me. She almost seemed use to the behavior.

I studied the card again. Something about the Amber Street address stuck a cord with me.

I knew this address.

I made sure to include Monique Sanders in my prayers. The young woman was disturbed. She had lost the man she felt would be her husband, watched a man she used to date with his bride-to-be and the man who'd been there all of her life was fighting for his life.

If I've learned anything in my sixty odd years, there was always evidence to be found that drove a person over the edge. It was often my most difficult students who had the most challenging home lives. Their time in the classroom was their time to get the attention they craved. Even when Monique dated Cedric, I sensed in her a woman desperate for love and attention.

I slept better than I did the past week. Somehow, I convinced myself I had a plan, and all would be well.

When I arrived on Amber Street, I understood why the address seemed familiar to me. The bakery where Carmen and I tasted wedding cake samples was only a few doors down. My mind tried to comprehend the close proximity, but I needed to push ahead. It was almost ten o'clock and I didn't know if my showing up without an appointment would help me.

I stepped in and approached the receptionist's area. A middle age woman with short-cropped salt and pepper hair smiled at me. "Can I help you?"

"Well, I don't have an appointment, but I met Anna Hudson last week." I pulled out the business card. "I was wondering if she was available today."

The secretary typed on her keyboard. "She doesn't have any appointments this morning. I can check with her to see if she can see you."

"That would be great."

I waited to see Anna's response. After a minute of

young woman's face. "You seem to recognize the real Mr. Randall."

Anna's mouth softened. "I feel bad for Monique. She's very needy, and she's always been unlucky in love, which only causes her to embarrass herself." She sighed. "After Darius spoke at the conference last Monday night, Monique rushed up to him like they were together, grabbing his arm. He snatched his arm from her and began to walk away. Instead of taking the hint, Monique went after him. They argued. Anyone near them could clearly hear him tell her it was over between them and she needed to let him go."

I frowned. I realized Monique wasn't the most stable chick, but the story Anna was laying out in front of me was cause for concern. I leaned forward. "Anna, I've seen Monique in action, even before yesterday's blow-up at the restaurant. Do you think she did something to Darius?"

Anna seemed to give my question some thought. "You know I tried to call Monique a few times on Tuesday. I started to invite her to attend the dinner we'd plan with Darius."

"What dinner? Where was this?"

Anna shrugged. "Tuesday night at Good Eats. A group of us, the conference committee, wanted to treat Darius before he left town on Wednesday. Everyone had a good time. If Monique had been there, she would have made everyone uncomfortable. I'm sorry to say, but I'm glad I didn't invite her. Anyway, Darius left before the rest of us. He said he was tired and wanted to rest for his flight home. He had to fly out again in a day or two to some conference in Las Vegas. He was a very busy man."

Good Eats. Charleston was the largest city in South Carolina. Was it really possible that the world was this small? Was it possible that I merely glimpsed Darius seeking out the same restaurant where he would join the committee for a meal later?

Darius lost his life in the early morning hours on Wednesday. "Monique knew Darius was staying at the Charleston Place Hotel. She had to know where his hotel room was located," I pondered aloud.

Kendall had provided his daughter with an alibi. Did he really get discharged at the same time Darius was killed?

Anna cleared her throat. "Mrs. Patterson, I'm sorry again about Monique's behavior yesterday. I know she loved Darius and wanted him to love her back. I've known her a long time and she's had issues in the past. I can't say what her state of mind was and if she did anything to Darius. I know I saw her leave the hotel in a huff on Monday night and she returned on Wednesday looking for Darius."

She stood up from her desk. "I really need to move on to other business."

I stood as well. "Sure, I appreciate your time. And I will take a look at these brochures. There's just more pressing matters going on right now."

Anna's mouth curved into a smile, but I noticed a sadness had crept into her eyes. "I'm really sorry again for all this. Hopefully, this time Monique will really get the help she needs."

This time. "Help as in mental help?"

Anna nodded. "She's been treated a few times. Last time, she stayed at a facility in Florida right before she moved to Atlanta."

After Cedric broke up with her.

I left Anna's office, thankful once again my son didn't

marry that woman. At the same time, I felt bad because all she wanted was to be loved.

Chapter 23

The last child to be picked up from the afterschool program was Amani. Instead of her mother arriving, Rosemary stepped inside the church fellowship hall to pick up her granddaughter. Before leaving, Rosemary asked, "Is everything still going okay with the wedding plans?"

I smiled, displaying a confidence I didn't feel. I'd not been in touch with Cedric or Carmen since the debacle on Sunday afternoon at the restaurant. I held up my fingers and counted off everything that had been done. "Bridal fitting is done. Cake ordered. Deposit down on the reception location." I took a breath. "Rosemary, I'm doing everything possible to make sure this wedding moves forward."

She gave me a wry smile. "You haven't changed a bit, Eugeena. I remember when we were kids, you were always the one to bring everyone together. I hope your future daughter-in-law knows how special you are."

I winked. "She's not so bad herself."

I returned home quickly after closing the church. I

climbed out of my car and noticed Amos stepping out onto his porch.

Was he looking for me?

I waved. "How are things going?"

He waved back. "When you have a minute, I have some information for you."

"No need to wait, come on over."

I let Porgy out the back door, while Amos came in and sat at the kitchen table. I poured a glass of water. "Would you like some water?"

He shook his head, "No, thanks."

I glanced out the window and saw Porgy turning around in circles. Since I didn't need to be concerned with my pup taking care of his business, I went to sit across from Amos.

I realized I hadn't seen Amos since yesterday either.

He seemed to sense what was on my mind. "How's everyone doing after our adventure yesterday?"

"Adventure?" I raised an eyebrow. "That was drama at twenty on a scale from one to ten." My shoulders dropped, "Sweet Mama's Kitchen had become a favorite restaurant for Sunday dinners, and it's been so long since I had us together on a Sunday. We're probably banned from the restaurant forever."

Amos chuckled. "I'm sure the restaurant manager understood you didn't invite trouble."

"No, I would have never imagined a scene like yesterday. For once, I'm keeping my nose out of Cedric and Carmen's business."

"You haven't called to check on them?"

"No, Monique's outburst towards Carmen was bad enough, but even after I warned Cedric to tell her, he still didn't. The woman he's about to marry was left in the dark. She had no clue who Monique was until yesterday."

I took a breath and went to the door to call Porgy.

I'd almost forgotten him. He raced inside as soon as I opened the door. "Got lonely out there or something?" Porgy stared back at me and then looked over at Amos before heading toward the front of the house. I imagined he was about to settle down for a nap. Something I could use.

"Oh, I need to tell you about my visit with Monique's friend."

Amos peered at me. "Still investigating, I see."

I held up my hands in protest. "This was pain free investigation. I actually learned a lot. Do you remember the young woman who was with Monique yesterday?"

Amos frowned. "Vaguely. Was she blonde?"

I sat back down. "Yes. One of Monique's longtime friends. According to her, Darius broke up with Monique a few weeks ago, but she hadn't caught the hint. I might say that didn't surprise me due to her past behavior when Cedric broke up with her."

"She also provided further proof that Monique is definitely unstable or at least has been in the past. Seems she tends to go over the edge when faced with rejection, and a few years ago, Monique spent some time in a facility."

Amos nodded. "You're thinking she killed Darius?"

"She had motive, Amos. They had a fight Monday night. He pushes her away and reminds her within earshot of others that it's over between them. Now she didn't show her face Tuesday because she was with her dad, but suppose this breakup had started to sink in."

Amos clasped his hands behind his head, his eyes focused on me. "So you think she planned to confront Darius, but it ended wrong for her?"

I tapped my fingers on the table. "Darius had to have a conversation with whoever came to his room. Wouldn't you think an argument could spill over a few days and end with someone arriving in Darius's room, wanting a face-to-face?"

"All of this is possible, but the only problem is nailing down someone else prior to Carmen's arrival. I had a chance to talk to some of the staff at the Charleston Place Hotel."

I gulped the rest of my water and sat the glass down on the table. "Did you? Anything interesting?"

"You were on to something. Darius was an early riser. He received the same breakfast everyday right around six-thirty in the morning."

"Did the person who brought him breakfast notice anything?"

"No, she didn't notice anything in the hallway, but she said Mr. Randall was on the phone when she brought his breakfast on Wednesday morning."

"The phone? Well, then Detective Wilkes should have the man's phone records. She would've connected with whoever Darius was talking to that morning."

"You're right, she would have made the connection. At least I hope she did."

"How can we find out?"

"That would be where my contacts come in."

I eyed him. "You have people at the police station who would share with you? How can you do this without Detective Wilkes finding out?"

Amos smiled. "I have my ways. In fact, what are you doing for breakfast tomorrow?"

I cocked my eyebrow. "Are you asking me out?"

He held up his hand. "Well, maybe it's time you meet a few people."

Meet a few people. I had mixed feelings about the sound of this. On one hand, it excited me to have the opportunity to meet other people like Amos, who had professional skills that I certainly didn't possess. On the flip side, it occurred to me that Amos had this other life, other people outside of who we fellowshipped with at church and in the neighborhood. He was letting me into the world where he'd spent thirty years of his life.

I smiled back. "I will be up and ready to go at seven o'clock."

Amos winked. "Sounds like a plan."

Chapter 24

I'd heard of Maggie's Diner, but couldn't say in all my years I'd ever set foot inside. The farther Amos drove his truck out of Charleston's city limits, the more I wondered where we were really going so early in the morning. The diner reminded me of a Waffle House, cooks were behind the counter slapping eggs and bacon on the grill. The smells were certainly inviting to my stomach.

I followed Amos towards a booth in the back and almost stopped when I saw two other men occupying the booth. I assumed these men were old buddies of Amos. His contacts as he called them. We slid into the booth, me first and then Amos. "Gentleman, this is Eugeena Patterson," Amos said to his friends.

One of the men smiled, his dark skin crinkled. "The budding detective. Heard your retirement has been interesting."

Amos looked at me. "This here is Joe Douglas, my partner for ten years."

"Partners, until I took a bullet," Joe said.

Amos grinned. "Best thing that happened to you. Joe

retired a few years before me and started his own private detective business."

"Really? How's that going for you?" I asked.

Joe shrugged. "It brings in money. Never a dull moment. You'd be surprised how often people want background checks or want me to follow a supposedly cheating spouse."

Amos leaned his hand in the direction of a man whose hair was completely white. In fact, if he had a white beard, he could have easily passed for Santa Claus. His wide belly seemed a bit stuffed inside the booth. "And, this is Lenny Wilkes."

For a minute I thought I heard wrong. "Wilkes?" I asked. "Any relation to Detective Sarah Wilkes?"

Lenny boomed. "My daughter, even better detective than her old man."

I peered over at Amos, who provided me with his usual wink.

I wasn't sure how I felt. "So, your daughter doesn't mind you guys interfering in her investigation?" I started to say old-timers but thought it best not to offend Amos's buddies.

Lenny shook his head. "No interference, just keeping an eye on the cases."

Joe added, "Good old fashion detective work is what we do. All before people relied on DNA."

Amos said, "It gives us something else to do, you know besides the golf course."

I knew Amos wasn't a fan of golf, but from recent conversations, Lenny had played with Kendall Sanders.

The waitress came to the table to see what Amos and I wanted. I ordered scrambled eggs and bacon, and Amos ordered grits, hash browns and sausage. The waitress refilled Joe and Lenny's coffee then returned with mugs and a steaming coffee canister for Amos and me.

After a few more moments of silence, I looked at all of them. "So, I imagine Amos told you about my future daughter-in-law, Carmen Alpine. She's innocent."

Joe nodded. "We're seeing that."

"Did you find out who Darius was on the phone with that morning?" I asked.

Lenny said, "We did. Sarah already knows and talked to the person."

I narrowed my eyes. "Who was it?"

"Anna Hudson."

"Anna?" I exclaimed. I thought back to my conversations with the young woman, only yesterday morning. "Well, she was on the conference committee. She told me the committee had dinner that Tuesday night with Darius. She could have been thanking him for being a part of the conference."

Joe nodded. "That's exactly what she told the police when she was questioned."

The waitress returned with our plates. As I dug into the fluffy eggs, questions whirled in my mind. I'm not sure why, but I asked, "You said that Anna was questioned. Do you know when?"

Joe placed his mug on the table and flipped through his notes. "Well, according to police statements, Ms. Hudson's statement was taken around noon. The conference attendees had finished the sessions for the morning and were sitting down for the catered lunch."

A chill passed through my blouse despite the cardigan sweater I wore. *That wasn't right.* "Before noon? Do you have the details of that statement? I mean would the police say why they were questioning her?"

Amos looked over at me. "Yes, they would have mentioned Mr. Randall's demise. What's going on?"

I placed my fork down. "I met Anna that Wednesday afternoon and she didn't seem to have any knowledge of Darius being dead. In fact, she claimed she'd been busy with the conference and didn't know anything had happened. But you said she was questioned at noon." I looked down at my coffee mug. "Unless the police told her not to say anything, perhaps it was an intentional omission."

I looked up to see all the men glancing around the table at each other. Lenny shrugged and spoke first. "It's possible my daughter didn't say anything about his death when she questioned Ms. Hudson."

I could see the wheels spinning in the men's head, probably thinking back to what was in the statement.

Joe added, "There were a lot of reporters roaming around the hotel. The hotel was trying to keep the murder quiet as they could with the conference going on."

Still something was stirring in the back of my mind. I didn't know why, but I had one other thing to bring up.

"Have any of you looked into Darius's past? Did you know he was married two other times?"

"I think I remember you mentioning it to me," Amos said. "What are you trying to get us to see, Eugeena?"

"Find out about these former wives. Were there any children?" I leaned forward. "One other thing that has bothered me was the Tuesday before Darius's death. I discovered yesterday Anna Hudson's office is only a few buildings down from the bakery. It would be great to know how friendly Anna and Darius were. Was he actually following Carmen or just in the neighborhood?"

Amos nodded. "Sounds like you're not just concentrating on Monique anymore."

"No," I said, "I think there is someone else who's been pulling the rug over a lot of people's eyes, and I'm really curious to know why."

Chapter 25

It took two days for Amos and his crew to find out the information I wanted. On Thursday morning, Amos sat at my kitchen table and laid out the new information. The more he talked, the more chilled I became despite sipping on hot coffee.

I interrupted him. "Let me get this straight. Anna Hudson was the daughter of Darius's first wife. Darius's stepdaughter. You're telling me during this marriage Anna's dad had full custody?"

Amos nodded. "That's correct. She lived in Charleston with her dad. Visited her mother during the holidays and some summers."

"That fits with her and Monique becoming friends in middle school." I shook my head, "So, Anna and Darius kept in touch somehow after he divorced her mother. Why?"

Amos moved the papers around on the table. "Looks like they weren't in touch again until Anna was much older. By this time, she'd lost her mother in the car accident. Police reports state her mother was the drunk driver in the incident. She caused her own death and the death of the family in the oncoming van."

"My goodness."

"This is a theory, but it's likely Anna's mom, Jeanine started drinking long before her marriage to Darius. I suspect that's why the father received full custody."

"But you're thinking Anna's been harboring some blame towards Darius though?"

Amos nodded. "It's possible, but it will be hard to prove unless Anna confesses. She graduated with a degree in accounting and pursued her career in a profession similar to her former stepfather, but there's not a lot to indicate any animosity between them. She grew up in a different household and saw him when she visited her mother. Doesn't appear to be much of a relationship."

"Still she spent her preteen and teen years without her mother," I interrupted. "That's a rare thing. What happened for her mother to lose custody of her daughter? Are we sure her marriage to Darius had nothing to do with any leftover resentment in Anna?"

"We don't have the woman's word, but we're looking into people who knew her, trying to track down what happened. What we do know is the marriage between Darius and Jeanine was short-lived and ended badly. In fact, according to the timeline, Darius started pursuing Carmen while he was still married. By the time Carmen was pregnant, Darius's divorce was finalized."

I frowned. "If only Carmen had known. She wouldn't have gotten involved with a married man, no matter how charming he was."

"I agree, and here's something else that stood out to me. Darius's third wife was only nineteen when they met.

They married when she turned twenty-one. She also was pregnant but delivered the baby stillborn."

"It's interesting how his second and third wife was rather young." I stared into my empty coffee mug. "How old was Anna's mother?"

Amos pulled out a photo from an envelope. "Thirty-five. She was older than him."

I took the photo from Amos and looked at the woman. It was almost like looking at Anna. Her mother's features were slightly older. "She was a beautiful woman."

I wanted to know one thing. "Amos, this is all great to learn about Anna's past, but how do we find out if she went to see Darius that morning? Where was her hotel room?"

Amos grinned. "That's easy. Darius was in 828. Anna was in 827."

My jaw fell open. I felt the swooshing of air hit my lungs. "She was across the hallway? No one checked her room?"

I was in disbelief. I stood from the kitchen table and paced. "This was planned. She lured him here to Charleston."

"Eugeena, calm down."

"She wasn't planning on Carmen coming by though." I paced up and down, conscience that Amos was watching me with concern. "I bet she saw Carmen go in and come back out the room scared out of her mind." I swung around, "I need to talk to Anna again."

Amos stood from his chair, sending it flying backwards. "What for? We've just come to the conclusion the woman possibly had motive and was close enough to Darius to commit a crime."

I nodded. "I'm still puzzled about Darius's appearance at the bakery on Tuesday. When I think back, it's like he wanted to tell Carmen something. But how did he know to find her there?"

"Maybe he was visiting Anna in her office a few doors down and just happened to see Carmen."

"That's why I want to see Anna. I want to know if Darius was really there."

Amos looked at me as if I'd grown something on my face. "I still don't get why."

I didn't know if I could really explain it to Amos. It wasn't like I thought Anna was going to confess anything to me. "She talked freely with me yesterday. If I can talk to her about Darius and how he treated Carmen, maybe we can get more from her."

Amos took a deep breath. "You know you and I have had some interesting run-ins with individuals who had no problem killing a person. This is one for the cops, Eugeena."

"But the cops aren't going to ask the questions I ask, and Detective Wilkes has made it pretty clear her focus is on Carmen. She never even looked into the woman who was across the hall from the man. I find that unbelievable."

Amos stared at me. "It seems crazy, but the woman was one of the conference coordinators. Her police statement stated she was busy with conference attendees."

"How convenient? She was busy the entire time." I picked up the program from the table. "The conference didn't start until nine o'clock. There was time for this woman to get away with murder."

"What do you propose we do, Eugeena? Do you really think you can just talk to this woman when you suspect her?"

I thought back to all the television shows I'd seen. "Is it

possible I can wear a wire? If I can get her to talk will it be admissible in court later?"

Amos slapped his hands to his head. "Woman, you have been watching too many crime shows. There is no way that would work."

"How would we know if we don't try? You said yourself she wasn't going to confess to the cops. She has them fooled thinking she was busy with the conference."

Amos let out a long sigh. "You're not thinking this through. What if it goes too far?"

I smiled. "That's why I will have you there with me."

Chapter 26

Detective Wilkes shook her head for possibly the hundredth time. "I can't believe this," she muttered under her breath. Amos was sitting up front and I in the back of Detective Wilkes' unmarked car. We were a few doors down from the Chambers Financial Group offices. It was about three o'clock in the afternoon and the sun was high in the sky. Despite the air conditioning blasting, I was starting to sweat.

I had made an appointment first thing Monday morning with Anna. She seemed delighted to hear from me. I told her I'd read all her literature, which I had.

Now it was Tuesday, approximately two weeks from the first time I met Darius Randall at the bakery. In a few days, it would be October. The wedding was three weeks away. I knew Cedric and Carmen had talked, at least that's what Cedric told me. Neither said anything about calling off the wedding. That was a good thing. I hadn't breathed a word of what I knew or was planning to do the entire weekend.

Only Amos knew... and his crew, Joe and Lenny.

It took some convincing with Detective Wilkes. By her

constant nervous chatter from the front seat and Amos peering back at me, I still wasn't convinced either of them were okay with the plan.

Amos and I had approached the detective last Friday afternoon, and it took her a full minute to respond. I wasn't sure if she thought our plan was ingenious or utterly stupid. When she did respond, I had expected her to say what she did. "You're a civilian, Mrs. Patterson. I can't put a civilian in harm's way."

I argued back. "But Mr. Amos will be there with me. All I have to do is make an appointment. We can both talk to her, and I can casually bring up the bakery scene and how Darius showed up. Amos can ask her the other questions."

I had looked back and forth between her and Amos, who still wasn't convinced, but had long stopped trying to argue with me.

Detective Wilkes' face was hungry to have this whole ordeal finished, but it wasn't in her plan to have some old lady get a possible suspect to say something incriminating. She finally caved, though I'm not really sure what convinced her.

From what I could tell, Detective Wilkes had backup. I wasn't wearing a wire. Amos was. The plan was for Amos and I to show up as a couple. That is, a couple thinking about getting married. We wanted Anna to help us with a financial plan. Seemed pretty legit to me.

I have to admit my nervousness was more from Amos and I walking in as a couple. *Could I pull that off?* I mean we weren't really thinking about getting married. That had never come up in any of our conversations.

Amos broke through my thoughts. "Eugeena, are you ready?"

I peered at my watch. It was time. "Let's do this."

Detective Wilkes swung her head around to look at me. "Remember, you're not interrogating her like a cop. This is just to get some information from her. If we think it's useful, I will question her. Got it?"

I nodded. I didn't need the woman making me more nervous. This was *my idea*.

Amos smiled at me as I stepped out the car. I took a deep breath and hooked my arm in his. We were really doing this.

Eugeena, girl, you're taking this retirement time to a whole other level. Going undercover!

Chapter 27

What Detective Wilkes didn't know is we had some backup too. As we passed the bakery, unknown to his daughter, Lenny Wilkes looked out the window with a cup of coffee and I'm sure a danish. He grinned at us as we passed. When we stepped inside Chamber Financial Group, Joe was sitting in the waiting room. He looked over his copy of *Time* magazine as we entered.

I'm not really sure why Amos thought this was necessary. Did they think the woman was packing a weapon?

I walked up to the same receptionist as last week. "Hello, I'm back with an appointment with Anna Hudson."

The woman smiled. Her smile seemed to widen at the sight of Amos beside me. He was looking rather dapper dressed in brown chino pants and a long sleeve white polo. His beard was groomed perfectly today. The man looked like money. Not that he didn't always look handsome.

We waited for about five minutes before Anna stepped

out of her office. She also beamed at us. "Mrs. Patterson, it good to see you again and this is..."

"My significant other, Mr. Jones." I surprised myself with how easy that was to say. My glance back at Amos solidified that he was pleased too.

Once we sat down across from Anna inside her office, she explained some of the same services I'd already heard. Her smile grew. "So, you two have plans for a future wedding?"

"Yes, we're still talking about that. Right now, we just need to get my son married in three weeks."

Anna's smile wobbled. "That's right. So the wedding is still going to happen?"

"Oh yes, I know what you're thinking after the incident with Monique. But you know nothing can really stop true love." I reached over and touched Amos. That was my cue to let him know it was time.

I looked at Anna. "You know there was something about Darius that still disturbs me."

Anna's green eyes seemed to sparkle under the light as she tilted her head. "Oh."

"A few weeks ago, we were at the bakery down the street, and he showed up out of the blue. I've been pondering how he even knew Carmen was at the bakery. Was he here? I mean maybe if he was here talking about conference stuff, that would explain how he saw Carmen go into the bakery."

Anna twisted her hands and looked down at her desk. She looked up. "You know what? He did come by. Was it on a Tuesday?"

"Yes."

Anna smiled. "I can solve that mystery. He stopped by to see Mrs. Matthews."

Amos inquired. "Mrs. Matthews?"

"Yes, our receptionist. Mrs. Matthews is a bit of a fan. She wanted her books signed and couldn't make it to the conference."

I was impressed. "So, Darius made a special point of signing a fan's book? I guess he must have changed. Carmen described him as being awful to her. Her parents were and still are devastated by how he influenced such a young girl. She wasn't even out of high school yet when he approached her."

Anna seemed to be leaning in now as if she was a little girl enthralled with a bedtime story. "How old was she?"

"Seventeen. And get this, he got her pregnant. Of course, by that time she was eighteen, but still, it was creepy." I was cringing inside telling all of Carmen's personal business to this woman. But this was the same woman whose mother was still married to the man while he pursued a young girl. The one connection we needed to make for Detective Wilkes was Anna's relationship with Darius.

Anna stared off into space for a moment like she forgot Amos and I were in her office. Amos eyed me before prompting Anna. "Ma'am, are you okay?"

"I'm sorry I know this must be a shock to you," I added. "The man was your keynote speaker. He was very good at what he did, but his personal life, not so good."

Anna's eyes focused on mine for a brief second before turning away. "People are not what they seem. He was good at what he did. He knew how to handle finances very well."

I nodded. "I guess so. He was a wealthy guy. Carmen mentioned he had money early, even in his late twenties. I didn't think accountants made money like that. Do they?"

Whatever smile Anna had plastered on her face, seemed to melt before our eyes. A crinkle appeared in her right eyebrow.

Sweet Jesus, I think I hit a nerve.

The room seemed eerily quiet all of a sudden. I glanced over at Amos to see if he noticed the shift. His hands were in his lap. He carefully lifted his finger, his way of telling me to tone it down.

I'd managed to nail something we hadn't thought about. Even though Amos told me to cool it with the questions, I had to keep going. The picture was starting to become plain as day.

"I'm sorry. I'm talking too much. I was a teacher. Every other profession makes more money." I cleared my throat, deciding to change the subject. "Have you heard from Monique? I know her dad would make sure she's taken care of."

Anna answered woodenly. "Yes, her dad has taken care of her. You know Monique and I became friends because we both didn't have our moms around?"

I shook my head. "I didn't know that. I'm sorry for your loss, but I can imagine it created a strong bond between you two."

"It did. Except..." Anna stopped whatever she was going to spill.

I don't know why, but my teacher instinct kicked in. Anna reminded me of one of my students who needed a caring adult to talk to about their problems. I responded, "I remember going to Monique's mother's funeral. Her father was friends with my husband. It's hard for a girl to grow up without her mother."

Anna's green eyes filled with tears. "I'm so sorry. I'm supposed to be helping you." She started moving papers around on her desk. "We should make another appointment."

Amos was slowly shaking his head as though he knew I wanted to keep going.

This woman's emotions were on edge. If I thought about it, even the first time I met her at the conference she had that look. The one where you've done something horrible but needed to go on with life as normal. She'd convinced herself that she could play her role as the conference chairperson, focusing on the conference issues and attendees.

Maybe in the back of her mind, Anna thought Carmen showing up at Darius's hotel room was fate on her side. But when her friend Monique showed up that afternoon looking for Darius, Anna probably realized this was not going to be easy.

I remembered how she ran off leaving poor Monique standing there. Did the two women even go out later? How could Anna have looked at her friend?

Anna probably pushed Monique to the brink at the restaurant as they both watched Cedric and Carmen together. A friend for that long, Anna would have known Monique's breaking points.

But what were Anna's breaking points?

My mind went back to Anna's parents. They were wealthy. Her mom divorced her dad and women like that didn't walk away without something. Or did Anna's mother already come from wealth?

Something told me that an ambitious Darius Randall went for an older woman for a reason, and that reason was what troubled Anna Hudson the most.

I didn't realize Amos was standing, indicating we should

leave. I couldn't leave now. I had a feeling Detective Wilkes was going to get what she needed.

I leaned forward and asked, "When did you first meet Darius Randall? You seem to know a lot about him. I bet you knew he was married to Carmen. Did you tell Monique about Carmen?"

Amos started coughing. He really shouldn't have since he was the one wearing the wire. *His coughing was going to mess up the recording.* He placed his hand on my shoulder. "We should come back another day."

Anna's eyes had locked on mine. "You're right. I knew him. He was married to my mother."

"Oh," I responded.

This was too easy.

Amos's hand remained on my shoulder. I turned my head to look up at him. I believe he understood what was happening because he stood still.

I turned my attention back to Anna. "He was awful to Carmen. What did he do to your mother?"

Anna's hand shook as she unconsciously moved paper and items around on her desk. "She was never really a good mother. Dad always took care of me. He claimed she wasn't mother material. She had some good points about her as long as she wasn't drinking. I was supposed to stay with her that summer. She called and told me there was a change of plans. A few weeks later, I discovered her change of plans was a new husband. As soon as I met him, I could tell he didn't care for her. He liked her money."

"Darius?" I prompted. From the corner of my eye, Amos quietly sat back down. I hoped Detective Wilkins was hearing all of this.

Anna continued talking as though we weren't in the room. It was like a therapy session. "Darius Randall was a user. My mom's drinking got worse, and I know he was taking her money. He finally left her, but she was never the same. My father said she'd married Darius on a rebound from him," Anna scoffed.

I knew I was on thin ice here. I wasn't supposed to be interrogating Anna. I had already made the connection that Anna knew Darius. Her emotions about the man were strong and bitter.

She didn't know me. *Why was she saying all of this to a stranger?*

I looked over at Amos who observed Anna as though she would fly off the handle at any moment.

This woman was going to let the police believe Carmen killed Darius. But Carmen had moved on with her life and was preparing to marry the man she loved.

Anna Hudson had not moved on.

To confirm my assumptions, Anna said, "You know what he told me? He said I looked just like my mother."

Anna had a glazed look on her face. Then, her eyes focused as if she remembered where she was and that she had two people in her office wondering if she was about to confess to murder.

Amos stood again. This time I stood with him. We inched towards the door.

My voice felt hoarse. "I'm really sorry, but we need to go."

Anna opened her mouth, then closed it again. Something took over her body. I stopped moving towards the door as I watched her face crumble.

She stood and swiped her arms across her desk sending the freshly organized papers, a paperweight, and her laptop crashing to the floor.

Amos pulled open the door and shoved me out of the

office, but not before I saw the blind rage on the woman's face. Had I managed to open a festering wound with my questions? Was this woman really falling apart at the seams?

I barely noticed Detective Wilkes fly by me along with two other officers.

Where did they come from? The woman hadn't confessed anything. Or did she?

All I heard were anguished screams.

Amos drove me home. It was hours later before we heard anything. Detective Wilkes showed up at my door around seven o'clock.

I answered the door. "Is everything okay?"

She stepped in and looked at me. "Ms. Hudson is okay. She's under observation."

"Oh no. Did I mess up?" Amos came up behind me and touched my shoulders.

Detective Wilkes shook her head. "No, you did fine. Some people can kill another person in cold blood and it doesn't affect them. Those are the true sociopaths of the world. I think Anna Hudson is not one of those people. She wanted to rid her soul of what she'd done."

"She did?" I responded.

Wilkes nodded. "She was ready to confess. You were the voice that chose to listen to her. You made a way for her to voice her pain."

"But she seemed to be okay with Carmen or her friend, Monique taking the blame."

The detective hung her head. "I'm the first to admit I focused on Carmen. I didn't look closer at others with motive. Ms. Hudson used that to her advantage." Wilkes looked at Amos. "Looks like you, my dad and Joe were all over this one."

Amos tilted his head towards me. "Eugeena isn't too bad herself."

Wilkes cracked a smile. "No, she isn't. Although, I would still like you all to let me do my job. You retired folk have too much time on your hands." She shoved her hands down her pants pocket. "I owe you guys. I wish your son and your daughter-in-law much happiness with their wedding."

After Wilkes left, I looked at Amos. "I guess I need to call Cedric and Carmen."

"Are you going to be okay?" Amos asked. "You look shook up."

"I am. I keep hearing that girl scream. She broke, and I kind of feel responsible."

"You gently gave her a chance to see she had to come clean with the truth." He held out his arms.

I welcomed the hug. I needed *that* hug.

Epilogue

A murder. A funeral. A wedding.

I smiled through tears as Mr. and Mrs. Cedric Patterson were announced. Family and friends clapped for the couple as they entered their wedding reception. I also let out another deep sigh of relief. The last few weeks were the most up and down I'd had in quite some time. I'm sure what I felt was no comparison to the happy couple's feelings as they stood before family and friends sharing their vows an hour earlier. Cedric and Carmen shared a few arguments here and there, but their relationship had never gone through the test they'd experienced.

A week before the wedding, I hosted a dinner that included Carmen, Cedric, Amos and me. We all agreed there were some positives from Darius Randall showing up in town. Even Monique Sanders' dramatic appearance on the scene presented a necessary challenge. Before they walked down the aisle as husband and wife, Cedric and Carmen needed to understand long after the wedding ceremony there would be many more challenges. Getting through the obstacles presented to them, spoke to the strength of their love.

Darius's murderer was behind bars. The television networks had moved on from the story. As usual, there was too much competition in the news. And, I was grateful because it gave us all a chance to find some normalcy again.

At least normalcy for some of us.

Kendall Sanders passed away a week ago, and I attended the funeral. Monique stood with her aunts, her father's sisters surrounding her. I was happy to see she had support. I couldn't make myself go up to her and say anything. What could I say besides sorry? So, I prayed for her peace and comfort. I prayed God would heal her spirit and make her whole. I prayed that true love — a man that would not break her heart or spirit — would find her.

I don't know why, but the entire day I'd helped plan was passing by fast. It surprised me to see Cedric and Carmen walk towards the dance floor to start the first dance. Soon, they'd be off on their honeymoon. Thank goodness, Cedric had the good sense to plan some much needed time away in the Bahamas.

Beside me, Amos placed his hands on my shoulder. I turned to smile at him.

"Are you happy?"

I nodded. "I'm overcome with joy."

He narrowed his eyes. "You seem a little subdued."

"This has been quite a journey for my nerves."

"Yes, it has. I'm sure Cedric and Carmen are grateful. I daresay you won't have the typical mother-in-law conflicts with Carmen."

"No, I appreciate all my daughters. My Leesa and my sons' wives."

"Good. Are your legs feeling good enough for a dance?"

I smiled. "I think I can handle a little dancing, Mr. Jones."

I stood and clasped Amos's hand. As we moved towards the dance floor, I caught Cedric's eye. He winked at me before twirling his bride. It was so good to see him happy. Carmen was beautiful. Her smile wide, eyes gazing up at the husband who truly loved and respected her.

The lights were low, and the melody was nice, though I didn't recognize the song. Amos placed his hand on my waist, which moved my attention to focus on his eyes. We'd danced on very rare occasions.

Amos's smile dazzled me despite the low lighting. "Have I mentioned we make a good team?"

"You have," I nodded. "We do make a good team, Mr. Jones."

"A few weeks ago, we spoke about becoming a married couple in that woman's office. Tell me, is that an actual possibility?"

I stared into Amos's eyes. For a moment, I didn't know what to say, and I'm not one to be speechless. "Are you trying to ask me a question, Amos?"

"Yes. I'd like to know if you would marry me, Eugeena Patterson?"

In a flash, I thought about how important Amos had become in my life. How he didn't stop me when I was determined to solve a crime. He stood beside me and, in many ways, protected me from my own foolishness. I thought of the one man I'd been with all my life, who for most of our lives together, we were more housemates than anything else. There was no such thing as adventure.

I smiled up at the dapper man who, I had to admit, had captured this old girl's heart. "As long as someone else is planning the wedding. My days as a wedding planner ended tonight."

He grinned. "Shall I take that as a yes?"

"Yes. I will marry you, Mr. Amos Jones." I leaned my head against his shoulders and closed my eyes.

About the Author

Tyora Moody is the author Soul-Searching Suspense novels in the Reed Family Series, Eugeena Patterson Mysteries, Serena Manchester Series, and the Victory Gospel Series. She is also the author of the nonfiction book, *The Literary Entrepreneur's Toolkit*, and the compilation editor for the Stepping Into Victory Compilations under her company, Tymm Publishing LLC.

To contact Tyora about book club discussions or for book marketing workshops, visit her online at TyoraMoody.com.

Books by Tyora Moody

CPSIA information can be obtained
at www.ICGtesting.com
Printed in the USA
LVHW042152280422
717483LV00004B/411

9 780998 456966